Lo

Chapter 1

Pam lay in bed staring at the bright red numbers on the alarm clock. As the numbers changed to 4:15, she closed her eyes, and in her mind she was that little girl sitting in front of Granny's big clock on the wall counting each time the pendulum gently swayed back and forth. This was a place of endless daydreams and wild adventures; the same place where Granny would sit in her rocking chair and tell stories about life, love, and pain. She opened her eyes and whispered, "Sixty." The clock's numbers cooperated with her command and quickly changed to 4:16. This had turned into a morning ritual, a quick escape backward in time, a place where a mere sixty seconds seemed to take an eternity.

Now, back in the real world, it seemed as though that same sixty seconds somehow passed so much faster and with far less adventure. Pam drew in a long, deep breath and held it. She tensed each muscle and body part that she could. Slowly exhaling, she systematically relaxed each body part from her tightly closed eyes to her curled toes. This seemed to unlock her brain somewhat, get the blood flowing; it was something that she had picked up a few years ago in a stress management seminar during law school and had used every day since. Instinctively, Pam glanced at the alarm clock as the numbers changed once again—4:30. The room was instantly filled with a soft mellow jazz ensemble. She took a moment to cuddle her pillow, squeezing it tightly between her thighs and kissing it gently with her soft lips.

"It's been too damn long!" Frustrated, she released her soft prisoner. Pam sat up in bed and slowly looked around the room. Her eyes carefully scanned each meticulously placed item on her dresser. She could vividly remember the when, where, and why she had gotten each item. Her eyes locked on a gold chain with a small gold nugget draped over her jewelry box. In the middle of the gold nugget was a small, round diamond. As the glow from an outside streetlight squeezed through the tightly shut blinds, the diamond sparkled as if to assure Pam that all would be fine. This was the last thing that her Granny had given her before she died and probably the one thing that held the most emotional meaning to her. "It's not much, sweetie, but you are the sparkling light right in the middle of Granny's heart."

Pam wiped the tear before it reached the bottom of her cheek. "I miss you, Granny," she whispered softly and slowly got out of bed.

Not unlike any other morning before a hearing, Pam made her way to her study to reinforce what she had already practiced and labored with for months. She had always been meticulous, almost too exact, in the way she prepared for a case, but this one was special. She had to be perfect—this was her coming out case, her "big day." She had worked long and hard for this, her first highly publicized case. Five long years as the "go get 'em" assistant prosecuting attorney finally culminated in a once-in-a-lifetime shot at legal stardom. Pam smiled. "I never thought that old fart would retire." He didn't—he died of a heart attack right in the middle of the courtroom. Anyway, now she was the one in the limelight.

Nervousness tugged at the pit of her stomach; she knew there were those that wanted her to fail. Fail—a word she struggled to keep out of her vocabulary, but one that lately seemed to creep into her dreams. She quietly pushed those negative thoughts aside as she quickly scanned page after page of information; it was evidence against a man who she had never met but still a man whose life story lay neatly stacked in front of her. Pam carefully recited key points and issues, trying to play devil's advocate, wondering which way the defense would try to counter her plan. She had practiced this game many times before and had all but memorized every detail of every document that lay before her.

Pam raised the cup of steaming hot coffee to her lips and gently sipped. She felt confident that she was ready to win her first big case and was patiently waiting, being careful not to seem too anxious by arriving in court too early. She had time to relax her mind and focus on the task that lay ahead of her. She began to reflect on the events that had led to the murder charges and indictment of Mr. Julius Dent, a prominent and very successful businessman in the local community. She remembered like it was yesterday, the phone call that changed everything.

It had been exactly ten fifteen p.m. when the phone rang. She remembered thinking that she really shouldn't answer it, but of course, she knew she would. It was her assistant, John Franks. He told her to turn on the channel twelve news; he knew instinctively that she would not be watching the television—she seldom did. Without saying a word, Pam clicked on the television and turned up the volume. John tried to tell her what was happening, but his words fell on deaf ears. Pam was awestruck with the news story, totally tuning out the voice on the other end of the phone line. When the news broke for a commercial, Pam looked down and noticed that she had hung the telephone up. "I'll apologize to John tomorrow."

Chapter 2

Julius gazed out of his office window trying to decide whether to stay at work or spend the rest of the day at home with his wife, Tiara. He smiled to himself as he realized that just being able to have a choice probably meant he could leave or do whatever the hell he wanted to do anytime that he wanted to. He paged his assistant. "Denise, I'm leaving for rest of the day. Have two dozen roses sent to Tiara, and see if they can be delivered before I get home…Oh…have them sign the card, 'Champagne lunch in bed with Mr. Big.'"

Denise smirked, saying under her breath, "Lucky bitch," and reluctantly proceeded with her boss's request.

Denise had been with Dent Enterprises since the beginning. She was a twenty-year-old part-time college student when she responded to an ad for an office assistant. She'd had no idea what Dent Enterprises was; however, she was extremely confident and had always been able to make a good first impression. She was five feet eight inches tall, 125 pounds, and very attractive. Although she was very well qualified for the position, she knew that her appearance would give her a slight edge over any competition. Denise, as always, had arrived to her job interview about fifteen minutes early. Inside the office, boxes were stacked neatly on desks, chairs—well, everywhere.

After standing there looking around at the mess for a minute, she noticed this good-looking brother trying to fix the copier. He had on a pair of jeans and a shirt that showed just how much he must have enjoyed working out. "Excuse me, do you work here? I'm here for an interview with a Mr. Dent."

The gentleman looked up from his work and apologized . "I'm sorry, I didn't hear you come in. Here, let me move this box so you can sit down." The gentleman walked out of the room and down the hallway. It wasn't until she sat down that she started noticing how very nice the furniture was in this office. She also noticed that there were some expensive looking pieces of artwork throughout the office. "Hmm," she thought, "this could be promising."

After sitting for a few minutes humoring herself on the prospect of maybe having a good boss for a change, a fairly attractive lady walked up the hallway and introduced herself as Tiara. "This is looking very good," Denise thought to herself after sizing up the competition.

"Ms. Raye?"

Denise stood up and extended her hand in greeting.

"Come this way. Mr. Dent is ready for you."

Tiara didn't say another word until they reached the office at the end of the hallway. "Have a seat, Ms. Raye. Mr. Dent will be right with you." Tiara turned and left.

Although there were a few boxes stacked around the office, Denise could immediately tell that this not only was the boss's office, but also that this boss had some help, probably a female, decorating it. "This is too nice," she thought to herself. This office was laid—from the cherry oak finished desk to the black leather chairs, all the way down to the fully set up wet bar—simply laid!

Denise sat patiently enjoying the feel of the cool leather against her skin. She was almost surprised to hear the voice of the man that would be her future boss. "Hello, I'm Julius Dent." Denise stood up, and though she probably was a shade too dark for him to see it, she felt herself blush from embarrassment. This was the same handsome brother that she had seen in the lobby earlier tinkering with the copier. He obviously had brought a change of clothes with him, because now he had transformed into this stunning man dressed in a double breasted gray suit, a steel-blue shirt with a white collar, and a gray tie.

Denise's long pause gave way to a strained, "Hi—I'm Denise Raye."

Julius sensed her uneasiness and laughed. "Oh, the guy at the copier, well—sometimes he just wanders aimlessly around the office with no real purpose, but he is very forgiving."

Denise thanked Julius for his understanding of her mistake and they started the job interview. Julius began by describing Dent Enterprises. He told her how he had started his company with one small nightclub in New Orleans. After about two years, he had added a restaurant, then another, and another. After much success, he decided to expand his business and move his headquarters to Atlanta, which was what brought him here. He had recently opened two very large restaurants here in Atlanta and depending on their success had planned to splatter his restaurants throughout the state.

"Now that you know a little about Dent Enterprises, tell me about yourself and why you think that I should hire you for this position."

"Well," Denise said and went on to describe her background in detail, from each part-time office job to her pursuit of a degree in accounting. She explained that she was taking at least a year off from school in order to save some money and then planned on taking evening classes until she could graduate.

After a relatively long interview, Julius thanked Denise for applying for the position and walked her toward the front office. As they passed the copier, Denise stopped. "Do you mind if I take a look at it?"

Julius motioned with his hands for her to have at it.

She opened the front of the copier pulled a few handles and out pops this wad of crumpled paper. Julius smiled. "So when can you start?"

"Tomorrow," Denise responded.

That was five years ago and Denise as always was still being the ever-so-faithful office assistant. Over the past several years, Dent Enterprises' revenues had grown ten-fold and so too had Julius's status and popularity in the local community. More and more Julius found himself depending on Denise for everyday office operations. He had to admit, she was very good and he never had to worry about her dedication to him or to Dent Enterprises. On more than one occasion, she had saved him from the embarrassment of forgotten birthdays, anniversaries, and the like, but most of all she seemed to genuinely care about his well-being.

Julius rewarded Denise for her dedication with frequent pay raises and bonuses, which not only enabled her to finish her degree but also allowed her to live quite well. She had long since decided to stay on with Dent Enterprises; her job provided her with everything that she could ever want, that is everything but the one thing that she could never have—Julius Dent.

Julius had made it clear from the beginning that he never mixed business with pleasure. In fact, Tiara had worked for him in New Orleans in the same position that Denise held for two years, and he had refused to date her—so she quit and they married a year later. This was the one thing that Denise couldn't understand. No man had ever been able to resist her. She never had to come on strong or be straightforward. If she were even remotely interested in a man, he would always come groveling at her feet; she always got what she wanted, until now.

Julius had no way of knowing that he was making Denise's life a living hell. He constantly showered his wife with gifts and praises of love, a love that he was not ashamed to express and frequently proclaimed openly. His weekly office lunch dates with his wife certainly didn't help douse the rage that was growing in Denise's heart. It was nothing that he was doing purposely; Julius was just being Julius. He had no idea that Denise had fallen in love with him, and on the surface, no one would ever have guessed it.

Denise never shared the fact that for the last several years all of her attempts at dating had failed. It wasn't that the men she dated were not good men; they just didn't or maybe couldn't match what she saw in Julius. She didn't want anyone to know that she was trapped in a world of want and desire for a man that loved his wife more than life itself.

Chapter 3

Julius sobbed quietly, "How could this have happened?" His mind raced wildly as he held his wife's limp body close to his. "Please wake up, baby—please!" Julius covered his wife's mouth with his and gently blew, hoping to bring back to life the only love in his life. Julius held her close in his arms. He longed to feel the warmth of her touch, the soft beat of her heart—but they were gone. Her body felt cold, and Julius instinctively held her tighter, trying his best to rekindle the warmth that had once flowed through her body.

Although he had dialed 911 only three minutes earlier, it seemed like an eternity. "What is taking them so long?" he wondered. Julius's mind was beginning to fail him. The seconds seemed like minutes and the minutes seemed to take forever. He didn't hear the sirens and certainly didn't remember letting the paramedics in the house. He felt suspended in time. He could only gaze at them, people he didn't know, sticking, probing, and tugging at the woman he loved. They hovered over her yelling things to each other that he couldn't understand. Then the pounding in his head started. Everything seemed to slow. He could see the paramedics' mouths moving but he could hear no words—there was no sound, just the pounding in his head.

Suddenly, calmness came over him. Julius felt a strange chill as if he were standing in front of an air conditioner. He put his hands over his nose and inhaled deeply. Tiara's scent filled his lungs—he smiled as streams of tears flowed down his face. Julius walked slowly toward the chaos surrounding his wife. He pushed everyone aside, leaned over, and kissed his wife passionately for the last time. "I love you, T—always." He knew that her physical being was gone forever, but her presence would be forever in his soul.

Julius hadn't noticed the police officers glaring at him from across the room. He only noticed the cocky swagger as they walked toward him with hands perched precariously on the top of their weapons. Julius looked behind him to make sure that there was no one standing there. He mumbled to himself, "Surely they couldn't be thinking—NO!" Julius pulled back violently as the one with the crooked mustache grabbed for his arm. It took all four of them to push Julius to his knees. They wrestled him forward and pushed his face hard into the carpet. They showed no mercy pulling and twisting his arms and finally slamming the handcuffs closed tight around his wrists.

Julius struggled to raise his head and screamed, "Why are you doing this to me?" As he lowered his head he turned to where his wife lay—that's when he noticed the small, thin cord tied tightly around her neck. His body shuttered then went limp. All of this was too much for Julius's mind to process, so in retaliation to the onslaught, his mind simply shut down. It went into a sleep mode to protect itself from further trauma.

Julius felt as if he were in la-la-land. He could barely recognize his surroundings and couldn't seem to keep focused on anything. It was much like being in a dream, a dream that he needed desperately to awake from. The police officers led Julius outside. They seemed to be surprised that the fight in him had gone and that he had no words to speak. Julius walked calmly past the crowd that had gathered in front of his house, and it seemed as if he didn't even notice the blinding lights of the news camera crew that came rushing at him. There were no words, no reaction, and for Julius, no sense to it all. It seemed kind of odd, but Julius noticed that the same hand that had been used to shield the top of head as he was put into the back seat of the patrol car, gently patted him on the back of the neck as if to reassure him that there would be no more hurt for him this night.

The patrol car slowly pulled away, inching forward through the crowd that had all but surrounded the car. Julius leaned his head back and closed his eyes tightly. The coolness of the seat against the back of his neck was soothing; it seemed to help bring him slowly back toward reality. But, instead reality came rushing back as he opened his eyes and caught glimpses of two men pushing and pulling a gurney covered with a white sheet, under which he knew lay the body of his wife. He stared back over his shoulder, looking but still not seeing that life as it used to be for him was gone forever. A love and a life, gone.

Julius reluctantly welcomed his mind back from its short stint in never-never land and along with it the cruel shock and disbelief of what had happened. He tried desperately to remember all that had happened, but it seemed the harder he tried, the more confused he grew. The only thing he knew for certain was that he would never have harmed his wife, and he also suspected that it would take much more than his word to prove that he hadn't killed her.

As they pulled into the parking garage of the police department, Julius braced himself for what he knew would be nothing less than humiliation and accusations of guilt. He knew he had to hold on to his sanity until he could reach his attorney, Bradford Broussard.

Chapter 4

Pam raised the cup to her lips once again and sipped. "Awful!" The once steaming cup of coffee was now cold and bitter. Pam looked up at the clock and proclaimed, "Showtime." Pam took a long deep breath. "This is what I've been waiting for." She carefully gathered her papers and readied herself to leave for court.

Pam thought that it was quite ironic that for such a big day, the drive to work seemed so mundane. She wanted and needed something to give her a boost. She pressed the scan button on her car stereo… "Hmm, now that should get my blood pumping." She turned up the volume until she could feel the bass vibrate her bones. Pam bobbed her head rhythmically to the steady beat. "Yes, just what the doctor ordered!"

Pam turned into the parking garage and quickly made her way to her reserved spot. As she pulled up, there stood John staring in amazement. He could hear the loud music as Pam drove up. Pam did a quick makeup check in the mirror and turned off her engine. John reached down and opened the car door. "Rap?"

"Shut up, John." Pam smiled. "Not a word or I'll fire you."

John just shook his head as they both erupted in laughter.

Pam knew that she would never fire John; he reminded her too much of herself—young, ambitious, and very good. He had actually done most of the legwork in this case. He had gathered all of the data needed and even sat in for her during the jury selection just like Pam had done so many times for her predecessor. Pam loved doing business this way; it prevented her from having contact with the person she was going to fry. She didn't want to be swayed by personality, appearance, or opinion, so she chose to keep her distance until D-day.

Pam and John quickly reviewed their game plan as they walked toward the elevator. "John, this case seems too open and shut. Are we missing something?"

"How many times are you going to ask me that? We have gone over every detail—we've missed nothing."

"Well, I certainly hope not. I…I mean we can't afford to give Brad any hole to crawl through."

"Yes, I know. If there is a hole, you'll find Mr. Broussard's head sticking right through it."

The elevator doors opened, revealing a long hallway that led to a pair of huge doors. John nudged Pam and whispered, "There they are!"

Pam looked up in time to see the back of two men as they opened and walked through the large doors. "We will see them soon enough," Pam exclaimed. She successfully hid her anxiety of meeting for the first time the man that she would attempt to prove guilty of murder.

In her mind she tried to picture an animal, a hideous creature whose looks alone could kill. John turned to Pam as he reached for the door. "Ready?" Pam took a deep breath and nodded. As the door pulled open, Pam noticed every seat in the courtroom was occupied. She walked briskly toward the front with John close in tow.

Pam's eyes fixed on the back of the two heads at one of the tables in the front of the courtroom. As she approached, she strained to peek out of the corner of her eye, trying to catch a glimpse of Mr. Dent, but John unknowingly blocked her view. They pulled their chairs out and sat as though choreographed and rehearsed many times before. Pam immediately arranged her papers neatly in front of her and made a conscious effort not to look toward John and of course in the direction of Julius Dent.

Pam looked up at the big clock behind the judge's bench. She gazed at the second hand first falling then climbing up each side of the clock. Briefly, she imagined that it was she that would walk through those chamber doors, adorned in a long flowing black robe, exuding omnipotence. "All rise." The bailiff interrupted her mini dream. "The state of Georgia versus Mr. Julius Dent. The honorable Judge Carlton Jones presiding." Pam was quickly jarred back to reality as the entire courtroom rose in unison.

Pam purposely stood further back from the table than John did to ensure that she would have no problem sneaking a quick peek at Mr. Dent. It wasn't natural for her to feel this curious; she never had in the past, but she just couldn't help herself—she simply had to look. Pam turned slightly to the right and was astonished to be staring right into the eyes of Julius Dent. For the first time in her professional career, Pam was caught totally off guard. She quickly looked forward, and on command from the bailiff, returned to her seat.

Pam was almost disappointed. She had wanted Julius to be some monstrosity from hell, but instead she'd looked briefly into the kindest eyes she had ever seen—kind, yet so full of hurt and pain. In those few seconds, she seemed to see straight through to Julius's soul. "What am I thinking?" Pam tried desperately to shrug off these unwanted thoughts infiltrating her mind. She remembered distinctively what her Granny had always said: "Always believe a person's eyes, honey; they can't lie—transparent straight to the heart."

Pam took a long deep breath, secretly going through her tension exercise, tensing then loosening each body part trying her best to hide her uneasiness from Judge Jones and mostly, her counterpart sitting across the room. She quickly regained her composure and glanced over at an unsuspecting John who was much too busy trying to look smug to notice Pam's brief struggle with her inner self. She relaxed and prepared for the business at hand—proving that Julius Dent murdered his wife.

"Counsel, approach the bench." Judge Jones motioned at both Pam and Mr. Broussard. Judge Jones covered the microphone with his hand. "Ms. Cooper, Mr. Broussard, I will not tolerate any showboating, arguments, or otherwise in my court. I'm warning you before time because my patience will be short and my penalties severe. If you are properly prepared, your case should not be one that keeps this jury away from their families and jobs for any more than one week. I do intend to maintain my reputation for bringing quick but fair justice. Do I have an understanding?" Both Pam and Brad nodded simultaneously, turned, and walked back to their seats.

* * *

Julius was concerned with the look on Brad's face as he returned to his seat. "What's wrong, man?"

Brad leaned over and whispered in Julius's ear, "He is looking for a quick trial—hope he doesn't already have the noose around your neck!" Julius looked up at the judge as he gave the jury additional instructions. He could sense by his body language and the tone in his voice that he was in trouble. He knew that he could not and would not have killed his wife, but how were he and Brad going to convince these people that he was innocent, especially if the judge already had him pegged as a murderer?

As the judge finished delivering his instructions to the jury, he prompted counsel to begin their opening statements. Pam stood up and walked quickly to the lectern. The silence in the courtroom was eerie as she stood facing the jury. She could feel her heart beat faster as the anticipation of what she was about to say loomed closer...
"Ladies and gentlemen of the jury, we are here today to do one thing. That one thing is to prove that the defendant, Julius Dent, is guilty of murdering in his wife, Tiara Dent, in cold blood..."

Chapter 5

Julius struggled to keep his composure as Pam's words penetrated his soul. His heart felt heavy in his chest. He cupped his face in his hands and cried quietly. He raised his head just as this woman who didn't even know him pointed in his direction—blasphemy, hellfire, and brimstone—the weight of the moment was just too much; Julius fainted. Brad reached for him but was not quick enough to keep his head from slamming hard against the table.

The courtroom gasped in horror as Julius's body started to convulse. The bailiff and several others ran to assist Brad with Julius. As they raised Julius's head, a steady stream of blood flowed down his face. Brad shook him gently trying to rouse him from his unconsciousness but to no avail. The bailiff screamed for someone to dial 911.

Pam's instincts kicked in; she ran to where Julius lay to give any assistance she could offer. She kneeled down and gently rubbed his hand. For the moment Julius was no longer the "beast that kills"; he was simply a bloody, broken man, a man that suddenly seemed incapable of committing this or any other crime.

Pam was amazed at how strong but soft his hand felt. As she stared down at Julius, his eyes slowly opened, and for the second time their eyes met. Julius's eyes seemed to draw Pam right into them—no words needed to be spoken; she could see and feel his pain. Julius's eyes closed again as the paramedics rushed into the courtroom. Pam, somewhat reluctantly, released his hand as the paramedics frantically checked his vitals.

Judge Jones pounded his gavel, ordering the court to recess until further notice. No one acknowledged the judge's action; all eyes were on what was happening on the courtroom floor. John noticed the tears in Pam's eyes and quickly put his arms around her and led her out of the courtroom. As they walked out, Pam noticed a woman dressed in black that was almost hysterical. Pam didn't have to ask; John volunteered, "That's Denise Raye, Julius's assistant."

Pam and John sat on a bench right outside the courtroom. Just as they sat down, the courtroom doors burst open and out rushed the paramedics. Brad walked briskly beside the gurney, constantly offering Julius words of encouragement. As the paramedics disappeared down the hallway and into the elevator, Denise Raye walked out of the courtroom doors, stopped right in front of Pam, and stared down at her through red-stained eyes.

The coldness of Denise's stare startled Pam and made her feel uneasy enough to grab and hold tightly onto John's arm. Without saying a word, Denise turned and quickly walked down the hallway toward the elevator. Pam looked at John and asked, "What the hell was that about?" "John, I've seen that look before, and that definitely was not just anger; that, my friend, was hate!"

"Sorry, Pam, obviously I missed something."

"Well, I don't know how long we have until we're back in court, but we damn well better find out what's going on before the judge reconvenes."

"I'm on it, boss!"

"John—I need to know if something was going on between those two, and I need to know it fast!"

"Pam, don't worry; if Ms. Raye was somehow involved in the murder, we will find out."

Pam sat there for a minute in a daze, trying to gather her thoughts. As John disappeared through the elevator doors, she slammed her hand down on the bench. "I've failed!" Pam knew immediately that she had relied too heavily on John to cover all the bases. In the excitement of this big case, she had concentrated too much on making the perfect presentation and neglected to make sure that the case itself was perfect. "Too late to fret," Pam whispered to herself. "This will give me some time to fix it." Pam got up and walked quickly down the hallway.

As the doors to the elevator opened, Pam looked down at her empty hands and realized that she had left her casework inside the courtroom. She walked back toward the big courtroom doors. As she reached to open them, she took a long, deep breath, then walked inside. Pam had never liked the eerie feeling of an empty courtroom, and after what had just happened, she liked this one even less. She hurriedly gathered the neatly stacked papers and stuffed them in her portfolio. As she turned to leave, she noticed something lying on the floor under the table where Brad and Mr. Dent had been sitting.

She walked over to get a closer look; it was a black leather wallet. Pam bent down and picked it up. "Must have been dropped in all the confusion." She opened it to see whom it belonged to. "Mr.

Dent." She quickly closed the wallet and placed it in her portfolio. "I'll call Brad when I get to the office," she said as she turned and left the courtroom. This time her walk to the elevator was slow and methodical. Her head was clear and her thoughts were focused on the tasks that lay ahead. She knew that there was something more to this case; she just had to figure out what.

Pam started the ignition to her car and was startled by the loud music blaring through the speakers. She quickly turned the volume down and pressed one on her pre-set channels. "Much better," she exclaimed as she pulled out of the parking garage and headed home. Pam picked up her cell and dialed John's office number. "John, I'll be in later; I've got some things to take care of."

"OK, Pam, I'm checking phone records, and then I'm going to recheck the evidence room."

"Good. I'll be on the cell if you come up with anything. Oh, get me Brad's number—Mr. Dent dropped his wallet in the courtroom, and I need to get it to him."

John gave Pam Brad's office and home number. "Pam, you were pretty shaken up earlier; why don't you stay home? I will call you if I find something."

"John, I think it's time to get my hands dirty on this one, but I will probably stay home until late evening. I will check with you later." Pam put her cell down and headed home. She took a moment to clear her thoughts, picked up her cell again, and dialed Brad's number. Brad's secretary informed Pam that he was at the hospital with Mr. Dent and gave her the hospital telephone number and Mr. Dent's room number. "I need to get myself together before I call Brad; I'll shower and change clothes first, and then handle that business."

Pam turned into her driveway and immediately started anticipating a steaming hot shower. She quickly exited her car and made her way inside. Pam plopped down in her recliner and sighed, "Feels like I've already worked all day!" She looked over to where she had laid her portfolio and thought of how she would love to search inside Mr. Dent's wallet to see if there was something she might be able to use. "No, it's wrong!" Pam got up and walked toward her bathroom, leaving a trial of clothes strewn behind her. She turned on the shower, waited for the water to get as hot as she could stand it, and cautiously stepped in.

The hot water was soothing against Pam's tense shoulders. She closed her eyes, lost herself in a sea of pulsating warmth, and for a moment forgot all the troubles of the morning. Pam reached for her body sponge and loaded it down with much more soap than she normally would. She closed her eyes and slowly lathered her body. Pam's mind quickly drifted to the feel of Julius's hand in hers. She dropped the sponge and continued to rub her body with her hands, quickly finding the place that suddenly was begging for attention.

Pam's eyes squeezed tight and her head jilted back as she found the place that her body was searching for. She opened her eyes and shook her head. "I can't believe that I've reduced myself to fantasizing about a man who may have murdered his wife!" Pam caught herself. "May have? Am I loosing it or what? This man did murder his wife, and I'm going to prove it in the court of law!" Satisfied that she had convinced herself to get back and stay on the right track, Pam quickly rinsed herself off and got out of the shower.

Before she could dry off completely, Pam had dialed the number to Julius Dent's hospital room. The telephone rang only once before someone answered.

"Hello."

Pam paused; she knew that the voice on the other end wasn't Brad's. This voice was a soft but deep melody to her ears. "Hello," the voice again sounded.

"Mr. Dent, this is DA Pam Cooper…" Pam had convinced herself to be firm and direct. "Is Mr. Broussard still there?"

"No, he had to leave town for the weekend."

"Leave town! Doesn't he know that the judge could call—"

"Wait—you obviously didn't get a call. Brad's secretary called here and informed us that because of the circumstances the court date was postponed for four weeks from today's date."

Pam clinched her teeth in dismay. "Oh, I'm not at the office, Mr. Dent, they probably left the message for me there. Anyway, the reason that I'm calling is that I have your wallet and was going to get Brad to come over to get it, but since he is out of town, I will track down my assistant to get it to you."

"My wallet?" Julius anxiously asked.

"Yes, I found it in the courtroom."

"Uh—I, well…"

"What is it, Mr. Dent?"

"They are releasing me in an hour, and I really need my wallet."

Pam hesitated for a moment, and then realized that this would be an opportunity for her to engage Julius in some candid conversation. "Mr. Dent, I'm really not supposed to have contact with you, but under the circumstances, and if you don't mind, I will have your wallet to you in about—say thirty minutes."

"That is very kind of you, Ms. Cooper. I would really appreciate that."

Chapter 6

Julius propped the door open to his room anticipating Pam's arrival. He walked over to the window, looked out, and wondered aloud, "When will it all end?" Thoughts of Tiara and the feeling of his world being turned upside down weighed heavy on his mind. "Tiara—only God and you know that I did nothing." The once clear, sunny day turned blurry behind Julius's tear-filled eyes.

Julius turned back toward the open door and was startled to see Pam standing in the doorway. He calmly wiped each tear at the end of trails that somehow seemed etched permanently down his face.

"I'm sorry, Mr. Dent; the door was open and I..."

"No need to apologize, Ms. Cooper. I'm just having one of my moments." Pam could see the pain in Julius's eyes. Looking at him standing there, obviously struggling to maintain his composure, Pam knew in her heart that this was an innocent man.

"You really didn't do it!" Julius shook his head no and again broke down in tears. Not knowing what else to do, Pam did what came naturally to her—she walked over to Julius and embraced him in her arms. Reluctantly, Julius allowed himself to relax and enjoy the warmth of Pam's body pressed tightly against his. Neither he nor Pam had expected to be in this situation and neither objected to this moment of heartfelt sympathy.

For the first time in almost a year, Julius felt, if only for the moment, that this weight he constantly carried had carefully and gently been lifted from his shoulders. He pulled away from Pam and looked deep into her eyes. He couldn't find the words that he needed to express himself—so he cried. Pam shook her head no, as if to reassure him that he need not shed another tear and pulled him close to her again.

Pam whispered in Julius's ear, "I know in my heart that you didn't kill your wife." Julius sobbed openly. He couldn't believe that the woman who had vowed to see him put away for life, was now consoling and reassuring him. "You have to trust me, Julius—you have to trust me!"

Julius nodded yes, and muttered a barely audible, "OOK." Pam led Julius out of the room and toward the elevator. Neither spoke a word until they were tucked neatly inside the elevator and away from prying eyes.

"Julius, you know that I could ruin my career by doing this."

"I know…" Julius stared at the elevator floor.

"Don't worry; I've taken far more chances in life than this. I just, well, I really hope that I'm right about you, Julius; I really hope I'm right."

Pam reached into her purse to retrieve Julius's wallet. After handing the wallet to him, she stared straight ahead at the elevator doors and jokingly exclaimed, "Don't worry, I didn't look through it!"

Julius caught himself smiling; the first real smile since the day Tiara died.

Julius agreed to meet Pam at her house later that night to go over everything that had happened the night Tiara died. Before the elevator doors opened, they shook hands and said goodbye.

Pam hurried to her car. "Thank goodness this is Friday; maybe it will give us enough time to dig up something that we missed." Out the corner of her eye, Pam caught a glimpse of a car turning out of the parking lot. "No, it couldn't be!" Pam wasn't one hundred percent sure, but she thought that the woman driving that car looked a lot like Denise Raye, and she was absolutely certain that the man on the passenger side was none other than Julius Dent.

Pam's heart sank to her feet. She slowly shook her head. "Mr. Dent, I'm not going to let my guard down; I will find out the truth. You bet your life I will." Pam got into her car and sped toward her office. Before she could travel three blocks, the familiar chirp of her cell phone filled the air. It was John.

"Pam, first let me apologize; it seems that I missed something paramount…"

"What?" Pam snapped.

"Well, actually, Pam, there are a few things…"

"Look, John, I'll be in the office in five minutes. Meet me there with EVERYTHING that you have found." Pam didn't give John a chance to say another word before she angrily pressed "end" on her cell phone.

Pam shoved the cell phone down hard against the seat. She was pissed; she just didn't know at whom. Somewhere between her seeing Julius in the car with Denise and John admitting that he had overlooked key information, her blood pressure had reached the boiling point. Pam inhaled deeply. "Calm down, just calm down," Pam whispered. She slowly exhaled, trying to release some of the tension that was overtaking her. "Don't get rattled, girl; got to keep your composure!" Pam tried desperately to talk herself down, and as she pulled into the parking garage of her office, she finally felt a little bit better.

Pam took another long, deep breath before she opened the door to the office area. She was greeted promptly by her secretary, Mae. "I didn't expect to see you in today. We were worried about you after what happened in the court room." Mae gave Pam a handful of messages. Pam rifled through the messages as she walked into her office. Looking at the messages, she could tell that John had been very busy. Before she could sit down, John walked in. "Close the door," Pam said in a calm voice.

John reached behind him and gently closed the door.

"Come over and have a seat." John walked slowly and sat down in the chair directly in front of Pam's desk. "John, before you tell me anything about what you've found, let me tell you how I feel about this whole mess. When I was in your position, I busted my butt to make my boss look good. It took a lot of long days and sleepless nights, but I never gave him less than my best effort. No case was unimportant; I treated every case as though it was my last chance to prove that I was worthy of being the DA."

"Pam…I'm…"

"No, John, let me finish! I never let my boss down—never gave him a reason to second guess me. John, you are my chosen successor for one reason and one reason only; you are good. But you let me down; you relaxed, got lazy, and now I'm in a very precarious position. If we don't get out of this one unblemished, I can't promise you that I won't take it personal."

"Pam, I'm so very sorry. I've been killing myself, simply dying on the inside because I know that I failed you. My job is very important to me, but you are even more important. You have been my mentor, my friend, and my confidant. I apologize sincerely, and I will never fail you again. I don't know if we can pull this one out, but I have been and will continue to work as hard as I possibly can to give us a fighting chance."

Pam's face was stern. The usual smile that John could bring out of her was missing. She was strictly business, and right now her business was to fix this case. "So, what do you have?"

"Pam, I've been at it since we left the courtroom today. I've contacted and interviewed some very interesting people. I've gone to the crime lab and rechecked some things—you won't believe what I found."

"OK, enough of the dramatics, what do you have?"

"Well, let me start with the crime lab. The DNA test results from the stains on the sheets were from two different people. The stain was a mixture of bodily secretions; one which matched Mr. Dent's DNA, the other was not from Tiara Dent—in fact the autopsy report indicated that Mrs. Dent did not have sexual intercourse at all that night."

"John, are you saying that…"

"I don't know, Pam, but it sure seems to point toward a third person being in that bed that night. Wait, there's more…there was something else that showed up in a blood sample drawn from Mr. Dent and from Mrs. Dent's autopsy—Rohypnol!"

Pam stood straight up and screamed, "Rohypnol! Date rape drugs—in both of them?"

"Yes—in both of them."

"John, what the hell is going on?" Pam sat back down in her chair and cupped her face in her hands. She simply couldn't believe what she was hearing—couldn't believe what she was hearing at all.

Pam's mind was racing relentlessly. She knew that Bradford Broussard would not have missed this information; she knew instantly that she was going to lose this case. Pam looked up at John. "John, we have less than four weeks to get our shit…" Pam stopped in midsentence and stared blankly at the floor.

"Pam, you OK?"

Pam looked up at John. "Denise Raye, she's the key; I can feel it! We have a couple weeks. Use all of your resources; find out **everything** about Ms. Raye. I want to know how many times she wiped her ass in the last two years!" Pam stood up and walked over to John. "Now, I'm going to concentrate on Mr. Dent. I will meet with him tonight. I will keep my cell phone on; if I feel that I'm in trouble, I will speed dial you and leave the line open so you can hear what's going on."

"Pam, let me handle Mr. Dent; that sounds a little too risky for you."

"Unfortunately, John, we don't have time for caution, and this case is too damn important. I'm a big girl; I can take care of myself. If I need you I will call."

John stood up. "Be careful; I will get what we need on Ms. Raye. I will call you at ten p.m. to update you."

She sat back down in her chair as John left her office. She looked through her notes for Julius's telephone number.

Chapter 7

"Denise, it was so nice of you to give me a ride home. You have truly been a good friend."

Denise looked over at Julius and smiled. "Julius, you know that I would do anything in the world for you; besides, who else is going to take care of you?" Denise reached over to offer Julius her hand and inhaled deeply as he grabbed and gently squeezed it. She thought, "Finally, he's mine." She was sure that Julius was ready to accept her as his lover, something that she had impatiently waited for for what seemed like an eternity.

Julius raised her hand to his lips and gently kissed it. Denise's heart raced with excitement. She tried to hide the fact that her legs were trembling, but the immediate feeling of warmth and moisture between her legs was almost too much to bear. Denise was ready this time; she didn't want to make the mistake of rushing Julius, so she quickly calmed herself down. "Julius, I know that you are probably still not feeling well, so I'm going to take you home and put you to bed. "I've got some errands to run, but I'll stop by later and cook you something to eat."

"You don't have to do that, Denise…"

"Shhh—don't you say another word; it's the least I could do!"

Julius smiled and said, "Well, I certainly hope you can cook."

Denise shook her finger at him and said, "Well, it's probably a lot better than that hospital food!" They both laughed as Denise pulled into the driveway of Julius's condominium. Denise felt somewhat awkward. She felt that she had her momentum going and was reluctant to stop now. She wondered if she should go inside and screw Julius's brains out or if she should just continue to play it cool.

"Denise, I'll leave a key above the door just in case I'm asleep when you come back." Denise was speechless; she opened her mouth but couldn't find the words, so she just nodded OK and backed out of the driveway. When she was sure that she was out of sight, she pumped her fist in the air and screamed loudly, "Yessss!" Denise turned her music up and sang aloud. She felt that she had conquered the mountaintop. "Everything was worth it," she said.

Suddenly it hit her. "What if they convict him; all of this is going to be for nothing! Well, at least he will still be mine… and for now,

I'm going to find the sexiest lingerie that I can, give him what I know that he has really wanted all these years—and this time I will be all that's on his mind."

* * *

Julius sat on the edge of his bed and smiled. He thought aloud, "Denise really has been sweet; she will make someone a fine wife someday." Julius noticed the scent of Denise's perfume on his hands. He cupped his hands over his nose and inhaled deeply. A strange sensation came over him. His head pounded as small memory flashes struggled to be released from their long held prison. Julius closed his eyes tightly and shook his head. "Damn, what the hell was that?" Julius knew right away that sleep would not come for him if thoughts of Tiara started bombarding his mind like a hailstorm.

Julius remembered that the hospital had called in a prescription to the pharmacy to help him rest. "I think I better go pick up that prescription, or I might not get any rest at all." Julius grabbed his car keys, and headed for the door. As he closed the door behind him, he heard the telephone ring. Julius had forgotten that he had taken his house key off the key ring and placed it above the front door for Denise and by the time he realized it, his answering machine had clicked on. "Oh well, I'll check it when I get back. It's probably Denise checking on me; she will just think I'm asleep. Besides, this shouldn't take that long; I'll surely make it back before she gets here." Julius got in his car. "I better take the interstate; it will be quicker."

Had Julius turned on his radio, he would not have taken the interstate. In between his house and the exit to the pharmacy, there was a major accident; traffic was backed up for miles, and before he knew it, he was right in the middle of it. "Damn, this is all I need!" Like everyone else, Julius stepped out of his car and looked as far up the interstate as he could see—nothing but a sea of cars was in front of him and the very same behind him. Julius looked in the glove compartment to retrieve his cell phone, but to his dismay, he had left it at home. "I should have just stayed my ass in the hospital!" Julius sat back down, rolled down his windows and turned on his radio. "May as well get comfortable—I'm going to be here a while."

Julius pressed his head back against the headrest. Again he

cupped his hands around his nose and inhaled; Denise's scent was as strong as ever…then, just like before, the flashes of memories. "Why is this perfume jarring my memory?" Julius cupped his hands once more and inhaled repeatedly. He closed his eyes tightly and for the first time since the death of his wife, his mind didn't fail him; the memories of that night started flowing through his mind.

…Julius lay in bed with Tiara. He marveled at how beautiful his wife was as she lay on her side. Julius lightly ran his hand from Tiara's toes, slowly upward along every inch of her body, being careful not to miss one spot. Julius teasingly inched his way up her silky soft thighs to that special spot that made Tiara take a long, deep breath. Julius was careful not to stay in that spot too long; he had plans for that very special place later. He continued his journey over her soft, full breasts and finally ended his journey with a long passionate kiss.

Tiara wrapped her legs around Julius's and pulled him down hard on top of her. She looked deep into her husband's eyes. "You make me so happy. I love you, Julius."

Just as they started to kiss again, the doorbell rang. "Saved by the bell," Julius laughingly exclaimed. "Now don't you move; I'll be right back!"

Tiara opened her legs and pulled her panties to the side. "Better hurry!"

Julius jokingly jumped out of bed and ran out of the bedroom toward the front door.

Julius looked through the peephole and was surprised to see that it was Denise. Julius looked down at himself and realized that he probably wasn't presentable. He only had the bottom half to his black silk loungewear set, and he surely couldn't hide that damn bulge. Julius opened the door and stood behind it. "Denise, what are you doing here?"

"Well, I knew that you had planned a little something special with Tiara, so I decided to take a chance and bring you something to add to the magic." Denise was holding a big glass dish of strawberries and a bottle of chocolate.

"Now you just go on back in there with your wife. I have to warm this chocolate for you; it will only take a minute."

Julius looked at Denise. "You are so thoughtful, or are you just trying to get another raise?"

Denise told Julius that she would go to the kitchen, prepare the dish, and let herself back out when she was finished. Julius agreed, and gave Denise a hug and a kiss on the cheek. "You go on back in there with your wife. I'll ring the doorbell once when I'm leaving. Enjoy the treat."

Julius thanked Denise and walked quickly back to the bedroom. Tiara was sitting up in bed sipping from her glass of champagne, "Who was it, dear?"

"That's Denise. She brought us some strawberries and chocolate—she's warming the chocolate for us now."

"Well, that was very nice of her."

"I know—we will have to do something very special for her on her birthday." After a few minutes the doorbell rang again. "OK, she must be finished. She said that she would ring the doorbell as she was leaving."

Julius jumped out of bed and hurried to the kitchen. Denise had prepared a wonderful-looking platter of strawberries. The strawberries were arranged in a circle around a crystal bowl filled with chocolate syrup. Julius looked over his shoulder to make sure that Tiara hadn't followed him; he dipped his finger in the chocolate and quickly stuffed it in his mouth. "Hmm..." Julius repeated his chocolate-covered finger, sucking three times before he finally took the tray to the bedroom.

As Julius approached Tiara with the tray, she asked, "Julius, what have you been doing?"

"Uh, nothing," Julius stammered.

Tiara burst out in laughter as she pointed out to Julius that he had chocolate on the corner of his mouth. Julius obliged her laughter by grabbing Tiara's finger, dipping it in the bowl of chocolate and slowly and passionately sucking her finger until Tiara's laughter turned into moans of excitement. Julius leaned over toward his wife and gently kissed her. "Tiara, I love you more than words can describe. Let's have a baby."

Tiara's eyes filled with tears of joy. "Julius, do you mean it?"

"Yes, baby, I think it's time."

Tiara wrapped her arms around Julius's neck and cried. "You don't know how much this means to me. I've wanted this for so long, but I didn't want to pressure you or distract you from the business."

Julius stared at his wife and with teary eyes said, "You are the sweetest woman in the world."

Julius moved the tray to Tiara's bedside table. He lay down beside his wife and pulled her over to him. Tiara put her head on Julius's chest. She whispered to him that she loved to listen to his heartbeat and how she felt that their heart beat was always in rhythm. "I love you, Julius Dent." Tiara noticed that Julius was breathing deeply. She knew right away that he had drifted off to sleep. "Well, that was fast!" Tiara gently traced her fingers along Julius's face. "Sleep, my prince—I will take care of you when you wake." Tiara sat up in bed. She untied her silk top, opened it, and stared at her stomach, "Well, I guess that won't be flat for long!"

Tiara reached over and pulled the tray of strawberries closer to her. She felt content eating chocolate-covered strawberries and sipping champagne until she too drifted off to sleep.

Julius was startled back to reality by the sound of horns being blown loudly, beckoning him to go ahead. He was happy to see that the traffic had started moving again, but he was disappointed that he couldn't sit a bit longer to allow his mind's eye to venture deeper into exactly what had happened that fateful night. Convinced that he had wasted enough time and that the pills from the pharmacy would just have to wait, Julius quickly took the first exit he came to, turned around, and headed back home.

Chapter 8

"Mission accomplished," Denise exclaimed. She quickly placed the grocery bags on the seat beside her and headed back to Julius's condominium. "Gonna cook some good food, put on my sexy shit, and rock his world!"

Denise turned up the radio: "AGAIN...THERE IS A MAJOR ACCIDENT ON I-75; TRAFFIC IS BACKED UP—TAKE AN ALTERNATE ROUTE."

Denise let out a sigh. "I'm sure glad I didn't get caught up in that! I don't want anything keeping me from getting back to Mr. Dent!"

Denise, knowing the city like the back of her hand, quickly navigated her way back, seemingly missing every light and potential traffic jam as if she were psychic. Denise smiled as she imagined Julius lying in bed patiently awaiting her return. She could vividly see him pulling her down on top of his chiseled body. Denise shook her head as the moisture and tingling sensation between her legs became increasingly stimulating.

As Denise pulled into the driveway, she let out a long sigh of relief. She had waited impatiently for this moment for years. "This time no one is in the way—the man is mine!" Denise grabbed the bags of groceries and walked toward the door. She was nervous as hell. "Denise, get a hold girl," she mumbled to herself. She reached for where she knew the key to the front door would be. "I'll be keeping this from now on." Denise opened the door and giggled as she put the key in her purse.

Denise took the groceries to the kitchen. "Julius," she called out. "I'm back." Getting no response, Denise smiled as thoughts of Julius lying in wait for her flowed through her mind. Denise walked quietly toward the bedroom, her quick short breaths indicative of the excitement she was feeling. Denise closed her eyes briefly as she anticipated seeing and being with the man that she had always loved...She opened her eyes. "Now, where is he?" Again she called out Julius's name; he did not answer.

Denise walked quickly from room to room searching and calling Julius's name. Finally she opened the door to the garage and saw that his car was gone. "Well, Mr. Dent must not have been too tired."

Denise closed the door and walked back toward the bedroom. She wanted to see if maybe Julius had left her a note or something to indicate where he was going. As she looked on his bedside table, she noticed that the light was blinking on his answering machine. At first Denise hesitated. "I really shouldn't listen to his answering machine, but it might just be that he had to leave, and he called back to leave me a message—yes, that must be what it is."

Denise convinced herself that the message was for her; she pressed play... "Julius, this is Pam Cooper. If we are still on for tonight, meet me at my house. The address is..." Denise was devastated. She could not believe what she was hearing. She dropped down to her knees and let out a blood-curdling scream. "That bitch!" Denise grabbed the answering machine and threw it across the room. She picked up a vase that was sitting on the dresser and smashed it against the wall. Shards of glass flew back toward Denise, cutting her on her arms and face.

Denise walked over to the dresser and stared at herself in the mirror. "I knew that there was something I didn't like about that bitch." Denise stared intensely at her reflection in the mirror. She took a deep breath, "Oh, but no... I did not come this far to lose my man to some stank-ass whore! I know that she is blackmailing him!" Denise wiped the blood away from her face with her hands and smirked. "Now I look like a warrior, bitch—time to go get my man!" Using the blood on her hands, Denise wrote on the mirror, LOVE TO DEATH

In her excitement, Denise had forgotten the address that Pam had left on the answering machine. She calmly picked up the answering machine, put it on the bed, and plugged it in. As she replayed the message, her eyes grew red with anger. She played it again...and again until she couldn't stand to hear the words any longer. She walked calmly out of the bedroom toward the kitchen. Denise grabbed a knife from the knife block on the counter; then she left.

Denise pulled out of the driveway and headed for Pam's house. Her eyes were glazed and fixed. She stared straight ahead and seemed to be on automatic pilot as she quickly reacted to each street sign. Each house that she passed was merely a blur in her peripheral vision. She was so focused that she didn't notice that Julius had pulled onto the street and turned into the driveway as she was leaving.

Julius thought to himself as he got out of the car, "She must have forgotten something." Julius was startled to see that Denise had left the front door wide open. As he walked through the front door, he could since that something was wrong. Julius carefully scanned each room as he walked slowly toward his bedroom. As he reached the kitchen, he noticed that Denise had left a sack of groceries on the counter. He also noticed that there was blood on the counter and that a knife was missing from the knife block.

"Denise must have cut herself. I had better see if she left me a note. I hope that she's OK." Concerned, Julius hurried to the bedroom—"What the…" Julius couldn't believe his eyes. He stared blankly at his room, confused at what he was seeing, but mostly afraid of what he was feeling. Julius's head pounded like a drum. He stared blankly at the red letters written menacingly on the dresser mirror. He could hear the words in his mind.

Julius allowed his body to fall back onto his bed, and then he remembered what his mind had wanted so much for him to forget. Julius closed his eyes and awakened the demon that had slept for so very long…Julius could feel the warmth of the mouth around his sleepy erection. He had always loved it when Tiara would wake him like this. He tried with all of his might to clear his head so that he could fully enjoy his wife, but he had never felt this way before. It was like his body wouldn't respond to his wishes; he just couldn't shake the drowsiness.

Julius remembered closing his eyes tightly as the silhouette of his "lover" straddled and guided him into the warm, wet depths of ecstasy. He inhaled the scent—but it wasn't the scent of Tiara. As the silhouette gyrated rhythmically on top of him, Julius turned his head to the right and thought that he could see his wife lying beside him. He thought to himself that he must have been dreaming; he knew that this couldn't be real. Julius could feel himself exploding in orgasm as the silhouette's movements had grown to a feverish pace.

Then Julius heard his wife's voice. "Denise!"

Julius sat back up in bed and wiped the tears from his eyes. "It was Denise—she murdered my wife—she killed Tiara. She must have drugged us—the damn strawberries!" Julius slammed his fist down on the bed. It was then that he noticed the answering machine. "What…" Julius pressed play.

"Julius, this is Pam…"

After listening to the message, Julius jumped up from the bed. "Shit, she is after Pam—I've got to warn her!" Julius ran to his car and sped off.

Julius's thoughts were as clear as ever. He knew that he had unknowingly pulled Pam Cooper into a deadly situation. He reached for his cell phone. "Now, what is her number?" Julius remembered that Pam had given him her home telephone number and that he had put it in his wallet. He retrieved Pam's number and dialed it, but there was no answer. "Come on, Pam, answer the damn telephone. Please answer…"

Chapter 9

Denise pulled into the driveway and stared at the large black numbers on the house. They matched the numbers that she had listened to repeatedly on the answering machine, the numbers that were still echoing loudly in her mind. There was no hesitation as she quickly got out of the car and walked up to the front door. She started to ring the doorbell, but reached for the doorknob instead; it was locked. She calmly pushed the doorbell and waited—no answer. She pushed the doorbell again. Still no answer.

Denise's hand twitched with excitement as she anticipated confronting the only person she felt was standing between her and happiness. She knocked on the door hard and waited...

Convinced that Pam was not there, Denise walked to the side of the house. She looked for a window that was halfway hidden from the view of others. "Shit, double pane windows." Denise continued walking around the house until she made it to the patio door.

Unfortunately for Pam, Denise had much experience at breaking into these types of patio doors. They were the same type of door that were on her apartment, and after locking herself out several times, she had become very familiar with how to get in through them. Denise carefully lifted the patio door out of the track, and just that quickly she was inside Pam's home. She carefully checked each room of the house, making sure that Pam was not there. After assuring herself that the house was empty, she sat down on the sofa and stared blankly at the front door, waiting.

* * *

Pam pulled alongside the car sitting in her driveway. She noticed immediately that it was the same car that she had seen Julius and Denise Raye leave the hospital in. Pam wondered why the car was empty. "He must have walked down the street or something." Pam walked to the end of the driveway and looked both ways; there was no sign of Julius. "I wonder where he is." Pam turned and walked back toward the front door. Pam had a funny feeling in the pit of her stomach—uneasiness...something just wasn't right. She reached for the front door, but pulled away as the sound of screeching tires filled her ears. Pam jerked around as a black car came to an abrupt stop in front of her house. The door of the car flung open and out jumped Julius Dent. He ran toward Pam screaming, "Where is she?"

Startled and confused, Pam struggled to put the key in the door lock. She was unsure of Julius's intentions and frankly, wasn't willing to wait to find out. Before she could turn the key, Julius grabbed her by the arm. "Pam, wait! Where is Denise?" Pam, still uncertain, reached inside her purse and secretly felt for the buttons on her cell phone. She pressed what she thought were the two buttons she needed to call John. She wanted to at least let him hear what was happening to her; what she didn't know is that instead of pressing *5, she had pressed *1, her one touch for 911!

Julius finally calmed down enough to explain himself to Pam. He told her that he could remember what had happened the night Tiara died. He hurriedly told her what he remembered. "Pam's hand dropped from the door knob. She couldn't believe what she was hearing; yet, everything seemed to make sense to her. "The Rohypnol!" Pam exclaimed.

"What?" The look on Julius's face assured Pam that he had no earthly idea what she was talking about.

"Blood samples taken from you and Tiara showed significant traces of the date rape drug, Rohypnol."

Julius shook his head in disgust. "That's why I couldn't remember—she drugged me!"

Suddenly the front door burst open and before Julius could react, Denise thrust the knife deep into Pam's side. "NO!" Julius screamed as Pam crumbled to the ground. Julius rushed over and pushed Denise hard. She fell over backward into the house. Julius knelt down beside Pam and pressed hard on the big red spot on her blouse. "I'm sorry, Pam. I didn't know."

Pam simply shook her head and then slowly closed her eyes. He tried desperately to stop the bleeding, but as he watched the blood ooze between his fingers, he knew he was fighting a losing battle. He could only look at Pam and think of how this couldn't possibly be happening again.

Julius was distracted by the wail of the police car as it stopped abruptly behind his car. He didn't say a word as the policeman ran, seemingly in slow motion, toward him with his weapon drawn. He noticed that it was the same cop, the one with the crooked mustache and who had shown him some compassion the night Tiara was murdered. There was no compassion in his eyes this time. "Stop!" the policeman yelled at the top of his voice. Julius closed his eyes as he heard the shot ring out from the weapon pointed precariously at him.

The policeman screamed into his radio, "I've got two down. Get an ambulance here now!" He quickly assessed the scene to determine if it was safe to put his weapon away. He checked the victims. "She will never make it—damn, she will never make it."

It wasn't long before the paramedics got there. "We have two victims—one with a stab wound to the right side. She seems to have lost a lot of blood—it doesn't look good. The other has a gunshot wound to the chest—I don't think this one is going to be salvageable." The paramedics screamed symptoms and vital signs into their radios and worked frantically to save their patients' lives. They did what they could, then loaded them in the ambulances and sped off.

Pam lay on the gurney totally oblivious to what was happening around her. In her mind, she was that little girl sitting on Granny's lap…again time slowed down; nothing was more important than what Granny was saying. "Sweetie, you don't belong here yet. You've got to go back; your work's not done." Pam climbed down off her Granny's lap and slowly walked away. As she turned to look back, her Granny was gone, but the chair that she had been sitting in was still gently rocking back and forth.

Four hours had passed since Pam had arrived at the hospital. There was a congregation of police officers, reporters, family, and friends. They were trying to keep things to a low roar, but obviously not being too successful. Pam opened her eyes. Her bed was positioned where she could see out of the half-opened door. She could see and hear the cop with the crooked mustache. She heard him tell a reporter, "If she hadn't dialed 911, and left the line open, she would be dead."

Pam smiled to herself. "I dialed the wrong damn number." Her smile left quickly when she overheard a reporter ask about the one who didn't make it. She heard one of the reporters mention Julius Dent; she automatically knew that he must be dead.

Pam's eyes filled with tears. She knew that Julius had tried to save her life and that the cop must have shot him, thinking that he was the one who stabbed her. Pam tried to lift her head from the pillow. As she did, someone placed a hand on her shoulder.

"Now you just lay yourself right back down—you aren't going anywhere."

Tears rolled down Pam's face. She recognized the voice immediately; it was Julius Dent.

"Shhh. Get your rest; we will have plenty of time to talk later." Julius wiped Pam's tears away and gently kissed her on the forehead as she quickly drifted away, succumbing to the effects of the sedative creeping slowly through her veins. He noticed how peaceful Pam looked and how much it reminded him of the last time he held Tiara as she lay lifeless in his arms. He cringed at the thought that this beautiful person almost lost her life, just as his wife had, because of him.

Julius's thoughts were interrupted by a light knock at the door. He looked over to see a familiar face peeking in; it was the cop with the crooked mustache. He motioned to Julius to come out. As Julius walked toward the door, he glanced back over his shoulder, making sure that they had not awakened Pam.

"How is she?"

"Resting. I think she's going to be fine; at least I hope so."

The cop extended his hand to Julius. "My name is Officer Mark Townsend. We will need you to come to the station tomorrow to make a statement."

Julius nodded his head in agreement as he firmly shook Officer Townsend's hand. He gently pulled him close and whispered, "Thank you." Officer Townsend simply smiled, turned, and walked swiftly away.

Julius walked back into Pam's room and sat in a chair positioned close to the bed. He leaned forward, carefully brushed the hair from her face with his fingertips, and gently kissed her forehead.

After a few minutes, he reluctantly left Pam's room. He hurried down the hall toward the elevators. Suddenly the hall was full of commotion. A group of doctors, nurses, and technicians nearly ran him over, pushing and pulling machines and blasting instructions at each other in a language only they could easily understand. With so much on his mind and his ever-increasing feeling of exhaustion, Julius dismissed the activity surrounding him and quickly made his way to the nearest exit.

Finally reaching his car, Julius paused as he reached to open the door. He felt as though he should go back and sit by Pam's side. He felt a sickening feeling right in the pit of his stomach—not just a desire to go back inside, more like a need. Besides, as he saw it, he was the reason she was here anyway.

After a few moments of internal struggle, his need for a long hot bath, sleep, and some good hot food temporarily took priority. He got into his car and drove slowly away, glancing repeatedly at his rearview mirror until the reflection of the hospital was no more than a silhouette fading in the distance. Julius sighed deeply. "What is wrong with me? Just can't shake this feeling; something is wrong!" Unable to pinpoint the cause of his anxiety, Julius continued his journey home...

* * *

Meanwhile, back at the hospital...

The room was deathly silent as the skilled surgeon removed the bullet from the patient's chest. Without provocation, a nurse carefully dabbed the sweat from his protruding brow. He stepped back, briefly admiring his work. "Close her up—I'm done." The surgeon's big brown eyes shown with glee as the rest of the surgical team gazed in wonderment at what had just occurred. "You see, near death doesn't mean certain death!" He exclaimed as he quickly pushed through the big swinging doors.

"OK, guys," the chief surgical resident blurted. "Let's polish up the good doctor's work." Immediately ten hands began working in unison, mending a body once lifeless and torn. Each hand reaching and grabbing in concert until the last stitch was in place and every unnecessary tube removed.

The nurses relayed vitals as they readied the patient to be transferred to recovery. "What's her name?" one of the nurses asked as they wheeled her down the hall.

"Don't know, but I think she came in with that stab wound victim."

"We'll have plenty of time to figure it out later. She will be able to give us all of her information when she comes to." The nurse checked the patient's vitals, IV, and monitors one last time, ensuring that the patient was stable before they left the room.

Chapter 10

Julius lay back in his hot tub. He felt drained as the pulsating hot water enveloped him and slowly began to relax every muscle in his body. He sighed deeply, "What a day." He slowly massaged his temples trying to further release the tension that had all but overtaken him and tried desperately to organize the thoughts that were still racing uncontrollably through his mind. Realizing that the day had just been too much for him, he closed his eyes and finally allowed his tired mind to rest. Almost completely weakened, Julius drifted quickly to sleep.

The door to Julius's bathroom slowly opened just enough for someone to peer inside. Julius was too deep into his sleep to hear over the soothing sound of the water jets bursting relentlessly in his tub. The intruder opened the door wider but did not enter the room. The intruder backed out of the doorway and walked down the hallway toward Julius's bedroom. She picked up Julius's shirt, the one he had worn earlier, held it to her face and inhaled deeply. As though intoxicated by the scent, she swayed then gently laid herself across the bed.

Tears filled her eyes as she rose from the bed. She reached into her purse and grabbed tightly the scissors she had taken from the hospital bedside table. She didn't flinch as the tip of the scissors sliced into the flesh of her fingertips; she simply walked slowly back toward the bathroom door. The blood from her bleeding fingertips dripped bright red blood and seemingly amused her as she stopped shortly at the bathroom door.

She took the time again to scrawl on the bathroom door with her blood "LOVE TO DEATH," then walked slowly toward Julius who was still sleeping and oblivious to his pending fate. She walked to the tub and raised the scissors high above her head. The blood from her fingertips dropped methodically into the churning water, then with one powerful downward thrust…

Startled, Julius jumped nervously, standing straight up in the tub. He turned quickly around to find no one there. He managed a half smile and a big sigh of relief once he realized that he had only been dreaming; however, the rest had cleared his thoughts. He quickly realized that the conversation he had overheard during the commotion at the hospital could have been about Denise still being alive, and if that were the case, Pam was in grave danger and he had to get back to the hospital quickly.

* * *

Several hours had passed, but the last time the gunshot victim was checked on, she seemed to be doing remarkably well. She had even managed to tell the nurse her name, Denise Raye. The nurses were amazed that she seemed to be so strong after what she had been through. Denise realized by the questions the nurses were asking that they had no idea what she had done, but that it would only be a matter of time before they did. She seized the opportunity to find out all she could about Pam's condition and, most important, where she was.

After the nurses had finished their rounds and left the room, Denise slowly pulled the tape from the top of the needle stretched across her hand and carefully pulled the needle out. She breathed deeply, trying to rid herself of the effects of the pain medication that had been creeping slowly through her veins. She cringed as she rolled to her side and attempted to sit up. Waves of pain shot through her body, but she was not going to let that stop her.

It had taken a full thirty minutes for Denise to gather enough strength to walk. She grabbed the scissors from the bedside table as she sneaked quietly out the room. Denise did not stop; she walked slowly and methodically toward the stairwell doors located at the end of the hallway. She never looked behind her as she disappeared through the doors. The only evidence she left behind were small droplets of blood that dripped rhythmically from the tiny needle hole in her hand.

She stared up at the seemingly never-ending stairs that zigzagged upwards—a mountain she was compelled to climb. With very little hesitation, she climbed the first step… Denise grimaced as the incision down her chest throbbed with pain. She stopped, took a half-breath, and continued, step by step.

* * *

Julius ran almost frantically to his bedroom. Without taking the time to dry his body he grabbed and pulled on the first pair of pants and shirt he could find. As quickly as he could, he ran to his car and sped off toward the hospital. He looked at the clock on his dash; it was three-fifteen in the morning. "I sure hope I'm wrong, but if I'm right, I hope I'm not too late." Julius sped as though, well, as though Pam's life depended on it. Julius thought that maybe he should try to contact the police, but he wanted to be sure. He would hate to have the police crawling all over the hospital searching for someone who was supposed to be dead.

Julius pulled into the emergency room parking lot. He knew that he would be able to get the information about Denise there. He tried to calm himself and while walking toward the emergency room nurse's station, concocted a story in his head. "My name is Julius Dent. A good friend of mine, Denise Raye, was brought here earlier in the day. She had a gunshot to the chest. Could you please tell me if she survived?" Julius glanced down nervously as the nurse flipped through page after page of a notebook on her desk. "Denise Raye?" the nurse asked. The nurse turned to her computer screen and started typing.

She looked up at Julius then back down at the computer screen. "Gunshot…to…chest…well, I don't have a name in the computer, but I do see that we have a Jane Doe gunshot wound to the chest…"

"Is she dead?" Julius blurted.

"Well." The nurse paused. "Looks like we thought she was, but I see here where we have her in the surgical recovery ward."

Julius couldn't decide what to do. "Should I call the police now are should I just go check to see if it's her?" Julius thought to himself. "Well, if she had surgery, surely she is incapacitated." Julius looked down at the nurse and said, "I know that it's late, but is there any way that I can just stick my head in the door to see if this is my friend?"

The nurse thought for a moment. "Just let me get someone to watch the desk; I will escort you to her room." Julius's stomach knotted up tightly as they walked briskly down the hallway and around the corner. Julius looked straight ahead, and though they walked briskly, felt as if they were moving in slow motion. He could feel his heart beating in his throat and the echoed pounding of each step he took in his bones. The nurse turned and looked at him as she reached to push open the door. Julius saw her mouth moving, but he heard no words—as he looked past her into the room, he could see the empty bed and the blood stained IV tube dangling.

The nurse must have seen the look on Julius's face; she snapped her head around and stared blankly at the empty bed. Without a word she left Julius standing there and ran to the nurse's station, summoning the charge nurse and anyone else who could explain the whereabouts of the patient. She and three other nurses ran frantically back toward the door where Julius had been standing—now he too was gone. The only person in the hallway was the custodian, slowly making his way toward the team of nurses, swaying his mop across the floor from side to side; washing away any evidence of where Denise may have gone.

The nurses ran toward the custodian. "Have you seen a patient wondering the halls?" The custodian shrugged his shoulders and muttered a barely audible no. One of the nurses glanced down at the floor. "There are blood droplets; she has to have been out here, and in the shape she is in, couldn't be far."

The charge nurse added, "And she's heavily medicated. She is probably lying in one of the hallways or has wondered into another room—let's spread out." The nurses took off in all directions looking down each hallway and into each room. Little did they know that right inside the exit doors, they would have found more droplets of blood, which would have led them straight to their Jane Doe, Denise Raye.

Sweat beaded on Julius's brow, and his hands felt cold and clammy. He looked up as the digital numbers above the door of the elevator changed in sequence: three, four, five. It seemed like an eternity; he pushed repeatedly on the button that already was lit brightly with the number eleven. Finally, the doors opened and Julius ran swiftly toward Pam's room, which was located at the end of the hallway two doors from the stairwell.

Chapter 11

Pam strained to see the clock on the wall. She rubbed her eyes gently, and then looked up at the clock again. She shook her head. "I've been asleep for a long time," she mumbled to herself. She snuggled back down into her pillow, still much too tired to resist the persistent urge to close her eyes. She stared at the bag that was hanging from the silver stand next to her bed. She watched as each drop fell slowly and splashed silently in the tiny vial. The methodical drip almost had a hypnotic effect; it didn't take long for her eyelids to slowly close.

Just as Pam's eyes closed, the door to her room pushed slightly open, just enough for someone to peer inside. Pam tried hard to open her eyes. "Julius?" she murmured. Through squinted eyes, she could see the door opening wider and wider. Pam closed her eyes tightly, then opened them again, trying to force them to focus on who was coming through the door. As she looked back at the door, it was closed and no one was there.

Pam chuckled to herself, "Me and my imagination," closed her eyes, and settled back into her pillow again. Suddenly, a hand slapped tightly across her mouth with such force that her teeth dug painful into her lips. Pam let out a muffled moan as the pungent taste of blood filled her mouth. Her eyes were wide open now; she could clearly see Denise Raye standing menacingly over her.

Pam couldn't believe her eyes. Denise was supposed to be dead; she simply couldn't be here. She tried to raise her head from the pillow, but Denise pushed down harder against her mouth and warned her through clinched teeth not to move. Denise put the scalpel close to Pam's eyes, taunting her, threatening her. Pam closed her eyes tightly until tears ran steadily down the sides of her face. She knew that it was her time to die.

Denise leaned over Pam, her mouth within inches of Pam's. "If it weren't for you, Julius would be mine. You will never have him!" Pam watched in horror as Denise raised the scalpel high above her head. She thrashed her feet wildly as the blade started its downward motion. Pam felt a dull pressure on her shoulder.

"Pam, Pam, wake up. You are dreaming." Pam's eyes sprang open to see Julius standing over her. She reached up and grabbed

Julius by the neck squeezing him so tightly that he had difficulty breathing.

"It's OK, I'm here, and I'm never leaving your side again," Julius whispered. Pam told Julius about the dream that she just had. Julius stood there in silence knowing that Denise was still alive. "Pam, she is alive."

"What the hell are you saying?" Pam shouted.

"They saved her, and now she is missing from her room. They are looking for her now. But, don't you worry, no one is going to hurt you, only over my dead body will someone be able to hurt you!"

Julius pulled a chair close to Pam's bed and tried to comfort her. He stroked her head slowly and gently. "Don't you worry," he whispered. "No one will harm you now." Julius stared at the peaceful look on Pam's face. He ran the back of his hand along her cheeks and marveled at how soft and beautiful she was. "I'm going to fall in love with this woman," he thought to himself. "I'm going to marry her one day—I can feel it." Julius continued to watch her carefully and rubbed her gently until she fell back asleep.

The door to the room opened. Julius braced himself; he fully expected Denise to step in and rush toward him and Pam. He was prepared to do whatever it took to stop her. A nurse stepped in and motioned Julius to come. Julius at first was very reluctant to leave Pam's side but had to see what the nurse wanted. Julius stepped right outside the door and looked up and down the hallway just to make sure that it was safe. "Mr. Dent," the nurse said, "we found Ms. Raye just inside that stairwell." The nurse was pointing at the doorway just feet from Pam's room. "She apparently collapsed while trying to open the door and was too weak to get up. She is dead."

Julius walked toward the door and pushed it open. They had already taken Denise's body, but scrawled on the inside of the door in blood were the words "Love to Death." Julius shook his head and walked slowly back to Pam's room.

Chapter 12

Julius slowly opened the door to Pam's room, walked quietly over, and sat down in the chair close to her bed. He took a deep breath. "Why?" Julius put his head in his hands and sobbed quietly. "Why did this have to happen—how did I not see this?"

Caught up in his moment of afterthought, Julius hadn't noticed that Pam had awakened. She lay quietly and listened to Julius think aloud. She couldn't help but to feel sorry for this man, and as reality set in, she realized that she had nearly ruined an innocent man's life—a man whose only crime was an undying love for his wife.

Pam's eyes filled with tears. "I am so very sorry."

Julius was startled to hear Pam's voice. Embarrassed that Pam had heard him talking to himself, he turned away and quickly wiped the tears from his eyes. "I didn't mean to wake you."

"No, let me finish. I was so very wrong about you. We did a poor job, which must have made things unbearable for you during a time that you were already in so much pain."

Julius, now overcome with emotion, turned and looked toward Pam. He wanted so much to say something, but the words in his mind seemed to have no meaning—so he smiled, turned, and quickly walked out of the room.

Julius paused as he closed the door behind him, turned, and stared at the door to Pam's room. He wondered whether he should go back inside or just leave this whole mess and wait on his day in court. He knew that Brad would not let him down, and with all that had happened, he should definitely be found not guilty. Once again, Julius cried, but this time, it was different. Julius felt as if the weight of guilt and not knowing had been lifted from his shoulders.

He wiped the tears from his eyes and walked toward the elevators. He could see a crowd of police officers at the opposite end of the hallway peering into the stairway. Julius quickly pushed the down button and waited impatiently for the elevator. He sighed deeply as the elevator doors opened. He ducked quickly inside, and almost frantically pushed the button to close the doors. Julius leaned against the back of the elevator and stared as the numbers slowly decreased—seven, six, five—and in his mind, he visualized releasing tension—four, three, two, one. As the doors to the elevator opened, Julius walked out with his head held high. He no longer felt as if he were in hiding and no longer doubted his involvement in Tiara's death. He walked confidently out of the hospital toward his car. "Time for Mr. Dent to get back to business."

* * *

Pam stared blankly at the door to her room. "Guess this one is over; time to throw in the towel." She reached over and grabbed the phone from the table next to her bed and dialed John's number…

"John, I'm in the hospital…"

"WHAT?" John shouted.

"Don't worry, I'll explain later. I need for you to call Judge Jones."

John was awestruck at what Pam was telling him. She instructed John to tell the judge that they did not have a case and that the state was dropping all charges against Julius Dent. She also instructed him to call the newspaper and release the same information. As Pam filled him in on the details of what had happened, his eyes welled with tears. "Pam, I should have been there with you."

"No, John, there was nothing that you could have done to stop this—the woman was obviously delusional."

"But, had I done my job, you wouldn't be lying in a hospital bed."

"Now is not the time for blame, nor the time to look back. We have a responsibility now, so we need to help undo the damage we caused Mr. Dent."

John got to work immediately. He contacted Judge Jones, relaying the information to him and asking for permission for an immediate press release.

Irritated, the judge threw a mini temper tantrum. "How in the hell can you call yourself a damn attorney, coming to me and my court half-cocked and making a mockery of the justice system? You go ahead and make your news release, but as soon as Ms. Cooper is well, I expect the both of you to make public apologies, or I will see to it that neither of you will practice law in the State of Georgia ever again. I expect full disclosure and will investigate and prosecute if there is any hint of inappropriate or unethical behavior."

John clenched his teeth and closed his eyes tightly as Judge

Jones went on a fifteen-minute tirade. After what seemed like an eternity, the judge slammed the phone down.

John took a long, deep breath. He pressed the phone hard against his ear and listened to the noise of silence…this seemed to help calm him after enduring his tongue lashing from Judge Jones. He thought to himself that he had probably ruined his career and knew that he had jeopardized Pam's. "Well, let me try to make it right." John scrolled through his contact list and started calling all of his newspaper and television contacts. This was huge news, and within a couple of hours, it was being broadcast as breaking news.

Chapter 13

Ink ran like mascara down the page as a steady stream of tears dropped methodically from her eyes onto the newspaper article. She woefully read and re-read the headline, "LOVE TO DEATH." Her eyes jerked from word to word trying to force her mind to accept what she was reading…the news that her big sister was dead. "What is this—how can this be?" After reading the full-page article repeatedly, Brenda sat back in her seat and wiped her eyes and nose with the sleeve of her soft cotton gown. She took a long, deep breath and slowly exhaled. "Now you can rest, Dee-Dee—now you can rest."

"Why are you crying?"

Brenda glanced up quickly and stared directly into the nurse's eyes and shook her head no. "OK, well, it's time for your meds." Brenda took the white cup from the nurse's hand and in one quick motion, tossed the pills into her mouth. The nurse gave her a second cup filled with water, and in one quick gulp, the water was gone. "Good girl!" the nurse sarcastically blurted as she turned and walked away.

As soon as the nurse turned the corner, Brenda calmly spit the two pills into her hand and quickly put them into her pocket. "These bitches think I'm crazy—they just don't know!" Brenda folded the paper neatly and tucked it under her arm as she walked back to her room. She held her head down as she passed the nurse's station, a routine that she had adopted to keep from having to deal with speaking to them.

"Poor child," one of the nurses whispered as Brenda walked past.

"Stupid bitch!" Brenda mumbled to herself as she shuffled toward her room.

Brenda took the newspaper and pushed it under her mattress. She sat on the side of the bed and rocked gently back and forth. She began to think of her big sister and how she had come to her rescue many years ago. She remembered how she had protected her from all of those who had tried to harm her. She remembered how she had kept her promise to always take care of her and to never let anyone know their secret.

Brenda continued to rock and recall the past—the past that was now becoming the present without the one person in the world who had really loved her. Brenda strained to control her emotions; she repeated what Dee-Dee had always told her, "You must always hide your emotions—never laugh, never cry, and most of all never let them know that you remember!"

"I'm trying—I'm trying really hard, Dee-Dee," Brenda whispered to herself as she slowed her rocking motion and reestablished her stern emotionless demeanor. "I'm going to make them pay, big sis—oh yes, they will pay dearly!"

Brenda's demeanor changed; now eyes red from tears of grief turned red with tears of rage. She bit deeply into her bottom lip to help squelch her uncontrollable urge to scream. She dug her nails deep into the flesh of her thighs until her nerves settled. With the blood that was now dripping freely from her lip, Brenda calmly wrote on the wall between the headboard of her bed and the mattress, "Love to Death."

She lay on her stomach with her blood-stained chin resting on her pillow, staring blankly at the words she had scribed on the wall. In her mind, she replayed every moment she had spent with her sister. She recalled each letter that Denise had ever written her, especially the ones that she would put a little perfume on and write, "Sniff here. See, Big Sis is so close, you can smell her." Brenda smiled as she remembered how her sister would always brush her hair as she talked about all the things….her mind exhausted, she fell fast asleep, but she hated to sleep—to sleep meant to dream, and to dream meant to relive the nightmare that would never leave.

As Brenda lay there, her face cringed as her never-resting mind battled the demons of her past. Her body writhed as her mind tried to deal with the pain of deceit, the reality of betrayal, and the memories of death. Deeper and deeper she sank into the depths of her subconscious thoughts, the place where that indelible line between sanity and insanity had become somewhat faded. As Brenda's subconscious thoughts and memories resurfaced, her body, just as before a violent storm, seemingly calmed itself, and just like a thousand times before, the dam burst, flooding her mind with reasons—reasons she had been forced to repress just to survive…

Chapter 14

At only nine years old, it was hard for Brenda to understand why her big sister was leaving. She cried uncontrollably as Denise packed her bags. "Dee Dee, but why can't you go to college here?"

Denise looked at her little sister. "Look, baby-girl, there are some things that I need to tell you about, but right now, I need to get away from here. Now, don't you worry, as soon as I get settled, I'm coming back to get you. Besides, Atlanta is just up the road; I will only be a few hours away and will come running if you need me." Denise grabbed her little sister, held her close, and whispered in her ear, "Dee Dee needs to talk to you about something…"

Before Denise could say another word, their father, Michael, walked in. "If you are leaving, you need to get gone!"

Denise stared angrily at her father as she held her sister even closer to her. "Daddy, I swear, if something happens to my little sister…"

"WHAT—you will WHAT?" her father screamed back at her.

Denise instantly recognized the look in her father's eyes and quickly backed-off. "Daddy, calm down." She knew that her father had not been the same since her mother died in a car accident a few years earlier. Denise stroked Brenda's long wavy hair as she looked down through tear-filled eyes. She knew that she was leaving her little sister to face alone what she had tried desperately to shield her from—a man who was slowly losing his mind.

Denise looked up at her father. "Daddy, you know that I have to leave for college. Why are you being so mean and hateful?"

Her father turned away from them and started to leave. Then suddenly, he turned back around. "Brenda, go to your room. I need to talk to your sister privately."

"But, daddy…"

"Don't 'but daddy' me; go to your room!"

Denise stared blankly. She could sense that something bad was about to happen. Brenda let go of her sister and ran hastily to her room, slamming the door hard behind her. Michael Raye stared at his daughter as he walked back into the room, closing the door behind him.

Denise stared at her father as he walked slowly toward her. She knew that unlike the many times before, words alone would not stop her father this time.

Thoughts of the day that her mother had died came rushing through her mind like a flood-swollen river. She remembered smiling as she saw her mother's bright red convertible two blocks away. Even from there, she could plainly see her mother's ever-present head scarf blowing gently in the wind. She remembered the joy she always felt when her mother would pick her up from pep-squad practice, and how the boys would always tease her saying, "Here comes Ms. Thang to pick up Ms. Thang!" People would always say that they looked and acted more like sisters than mother and daughter.

Then, as if it were in slow motion, it happened. Denise actually started screaming and running toward her mother's oncoming car before the accident actually happened. She could see that the speeding truck was not going to stop for the stop sign. She could vividly remember the impact—seeing her mother's head violently crash into the truck's bumper…then the sound of her mother's car horn blasting uncontrollably as her broken body pressed awkwardly against the steering wheel. As Denise reached the car, she knew right away that her mother was dead, her head all but severed from her body.

By now Denise's friends were surrounding her and pulling her away from her mother's mangled, lifeless body. Her mind faded to black. She did not remember the howling moans of the fire engines nor did she remember the paramedics tending to her; she only remembered the sound of her father's calm voice prodding her to open her eyes. As Denise slowly came to, she felt totally oblivious to what was happening around her. Her eyes met her father's, and without a word, he picked her up and carried her to his car. He placed her gently in the back seat and kissed her on the top of her head. "Baby, we have to pick up your little sister." Denise stared at her father as he walked around the front of the car. He paused and stared as the tow truck driver hastily swept glass from the middle of the street. "How could you leave me like this? What am I supposed to do now?" Michael Raye sobbed quietly as he got into his car and drove home.

Denise remembered that this was the last time that her father had looked at her and treated her like she was his fifteen-year-old daughter. Things changed very rapidly after her mother's funeral. During the next two years, Denise quit all of her extracurricular activities at school so that she could help with the house and take care of her little sister. She did all of the things that her mother would do to help keep the house running smoothly. It was a constant struggle trying to maintain her grades at school and tending to Brenda, but mostly, dealing with the changes in her father who seemed to be losing touch with reality. More and more each day he would mistakenly call her by her mother's name, and more and more each day he would exhibit behaviors that a father should never cast toward his daughter. A few stern words would snap him back to reality and things would quickly return to as close to normal as possible—that wasn't working now.

Denise screamed loudly as her father tossed her violently against the headboard of the bed.

"You think that you are going to leave me—just like your damn mother did!" Michael Raye raised his fist high above his head and brought it down hard against Denise's face. The blow sent her head crashing against the headboard. Denise screamed out in pain as her father unleashed the beast that she had, until now, been able to calm. Her father picked her up and tossed her to the floor. Denise screamed out loudly as her father walked toward her. She could taste the blood running from her nose and could feel the searing pain from the beating she had just endured. Growing groggy and weak, she looked up at her father as he stood over her. She noticed the door slowly opening behind him; she could see her little sister, staring at her with tears streaming down her face.

Michael turned toward Brenda and screamed, "I told you to get your ass to your room!" He walked quickly over to Brenda and slapped her hard across the face. The blow slammed Brenda's head against the door and knocked her unconscious. Denise stared at her little sister's limp body, Brenda's pants wet from urine. Seeing this made the adrenaline rush through her body, forcing her to forget about her own pain and giving her the strength she needed to protect her little sister. Denise grabbed the letter opener from her bedside table and ran toward her father. Just as he was turning around to face her, she thrust the letter opener deep into his neck.

Michael Raye stared at his daughter. His eyes no longer had the glare of a mad man. His light brown eyes glowed with the love and care that they used to, before his wife died. He dropped to his knees and smiled at Denise as if to say thank you, I'm free. Blood gushed from his neck as he sat down on the floor against the bed. Denise grabbed the phone and frantically dialed 911—she fainted before she could say a word.

"Hello, what is your emergency…?" the 911 operator repeated three times before she dispatched an officer. "We have some type of emergency at 50 Pinedale Circle. I think I can hear someone moving around. It may be an accidental dialing by a kid."

The distinct crackle and response of a police radio quickly responded, "Ten four, on my way." Within four minutes the officer was pounding on the front door; there was no answer. He walked to the side of the house and looked through a side window—he screamed loudly into his radio for back-up and an ambulance. The officer ran back toward the front of the house. By this time, the sound of blaring sirens could be heard growing quickly nearer. Two squad cars tore into the circle with an ambulance tailing closely behind. The officer ran toward his arriving back-up.

"I looked through the window on the left side of the house. There is a child lying motionless on the floor near the door and I could only see the top of the head of what appears to be an adult male sitting on the other side of the bed." Knowing that a child was involved, the officers quickly decided to kick the front door in and enter the house. The officers were very careful and cautious; they didn't know what had happened or if there was someone else hiding inside.

Weapons drawn, the officers walked strategically toward the front door, but as they were reaching for the door knob, it began to turn. They frantically positioned themselves ready to fire their weapons. As the door opened they saw a teenage girl holding a younger child in her arms. Both had blood and bruises on their faces. The older child obviously had suffered a fairly brutal attack. The officer closest to them quickly holstered his weapon, ran and grabbed Brenda from Denise's arms, and ran with her toward the ambulance. One of the other officers grabbed Denise's arm and ran with her toward the ambulance as the third officer kneeled in front of the door with his weapon drawn and ready to fire. The officers quickly questioned Denise on what had happened. She explained that her father had snapped and had started beating them. She told them that she had to stab him after he struck her little sister again.

With the girls safely in the ambulance, the three officers entered the home and made their way toward the second bedroom. Although Denise had told them that no one else was in the home, they were very cautious and careful, and searched and cleared each room and area before they reached Denise's bedroom. They called out, "Mr. Raye..." He did not respond. They called to him again, "Mr. Raye..." Still, no response.

The officer that had reached the home first motioned that he was going to approach. He walked slowly toward Michael, his .45 caliber loaded, cocked, and ready. As he got closer, he noticed that the carpet area surrounding Michael was completely soaked with blood; he knew instinctively that Mr. Raye would be dead. As he reached the body, he could see the end of the letter opener protruding from the right side of his neck. He kneeled down to take a closer look, turned, and looked at the other two officers who had now holstered their weapons. "He's dead." The officer shook his head and exclaimed, "This is a damn shame, just a damn shame!"

As the officers walked back through the home toward the front door, it dawned on them that these were the same girls who lost their mother in the car accident a few years earlier in front of the high school. "Shit! How do they recover from this?" One of the officers wiped a tear from his eye as he thought about his own daughters.

By now, the streets were full of neighbors and onlookers trying to figure out what was going on. The ambulance had already taken Denise and Brenda to the hospital. The chief of police arrived and was being briefed by the officer that first responded to the 911 call. Of course, this was big news in Valdosta. Other than the military base and the occasional robbery or domestic violence call, this place was pretty mundane, so the news of what happened had spread rather quickly. The chief decided that they would not give the media any information until after the girls had been officially questioned, so all that the neighbors and onlookers could do was wonder what had happened.

There was an eerie silence as the coroner drove slowly through the crowded street and parked in front of the house. The coroner stepped out of his vehicle and walked briskly toward the officers who were standing at the front door of the house. "What do we have, guys?" The coroner paused. "Other than just a dead person." One of the officers turned away and lowered his head. Sensing his disturbed demeanor, the coroner patted the officer lightly on his shoulder. "It's never easy. Just try to keep death in its place and…"

"It's not the death," the officer replied. "It's just that those poor kids have lost both parents now. It's just sad." As the officers explained the situation, they disappeared into the house. It did not take long for the coroner to make his official ruling that Michael Raye was indeed dead.

The Chief made his way over to the officers and the coroner as they walked out of the house. "Just take some pictures of the scene. It's quite obvious what has happened. I'll brief the DA as soon as we get statements. Someone get child protection services over to the hospital right now!"

* * *

Denise leaned over and kissed her little sister on the forehead and whispered, "Wake up, baby-girl."

Brenda slowly opened her eyes and smiled at her sister. "Dee-Dee, daddy hurt you; your face is…"

"Shhh." Denise placed her finger lightly on Brenda's lip and whispered, "I need for you to listen to your big sister now. We must have some big-girl talk, and I need you to really, really pay attention to me—OK?"

Brenda nodded in agreement as her sister continued. "Do you remember what happened?"

"Yes," Brenda whispered back. "Daddy was hitting you and…" Brenda looked puzzled. "…and." This was all that Brenda's mind would allow her to remember. "And then I saw daddy sitting on the floor…and he was bleeding—is daddy…?"

Denise stopped Brenda before she could say another word. "Listen to me. Daddy was trying to hurt us and I had to stop him. Sweetie, daddy is with mommy now—and he is very happy there, but we have to make a promise to each other."

"But…"

"No buts, just listen to me. Can you hear those people talking in the hallway?" Brenda nodded her head yes. "They are going to try to get you to talk to them about what happened, and then they will try to take you away to live with strangers." Brenda's eyes quickly filled with tears. "Don't cry. Big sis will tell you what to do." Denise explained to her little sister as quickly as possible what child protective services was and how she would get lost in the foster care system and possibly never see her big sister again. She convinced her sister that when anyone spoke to her, she would just stare and never say a word to them, and they would put her in a special place where Denise could come to visit her whenever she wanted to and they would always know where each other was. Denise promised her that she would come back to get her as soon as she could.

The plan worked, but maybe too well. In the beginning, Brenda played her role, but what Denise did not know was that although her little sister was dazed, she had not been knocked unconscious by her father; she had seen and eventually remembered everything, and it replayed in her mind over and over again, forcing her to deal with the pain of death all alone. What Denise thought was their plan to fool the authorities to keep her sister from being pushed around and abused by a system that really didn't give a damn about children like them, in reality, put her exactly where she needed to be, in an institution.

For nine years Brenda's mind was thought to be mostly dormant. She only trusted and responded to her big sister, and their relationship was one of trust and admiration for each other. Denise was very loyal and dedicated to her little sister, making the trip from Atlanta to Valdosta every two weeks, rain or shine, and writing her almost every single day. Denise taught her sister everything, ensuring that she was mentally stimulated. She would bring her college work with her and during her visits, would teach Brenda as she studied herself. While the staff at the facility thought Brenda was not progressing, she was flourishing, and her mind had grown sharp and calculating. She had learned ways to help hide what she was thinking or feeling and there was no one who could penetrate the shield that she had built around herself. Now, it was just a matter of time before she would force them to let her leave.

Chapter 15

Julius stared at the reflection of himself behind the words written so menacingly on his mirror. He momentarily hated the sight of himself and what those words, "LOVE TO DEATH," had represented. Julius turned away and walked from the room, returning with a wet towel. He slowly wiped away each blood-stained letter and with each letter disappearing, tried to erase the pain and sorrow that had somehow infiltrated his life. As he wiped away the last stain, he caught himself humming. He stopped and smiled as he stared at himself in the mirror; he was humming just as Tiara did when she was cleaning. Julius was somewhat startled as he realized that for the first time, he smiled instead of cried when he thought of his wife.

Julius sat down on the end of the bed, and stared at the picture of him and Tiara on the bedroom wall. "Baby, you know how much I love you. I always will. I have to try and move on with my life, so please forgive me for not being able to protect you, and please give me your blessing to live and love again." Julius closed his eyes and lay back on the bed. He just wanted to capture this moment, because he knew in his heart that Tiara would only want the best for him and would not fault him for anything.

Julius opened his eyes and got up from the bed. He walked over and took the picture off the wall. He walked toward his living room and placed the picture on the mantel above the fireplace. "You will always be the fire deep in my heart, and my passions will always reflect the love that I have for you." Julius smiled once again as he turned and walked away.

As Julius walked back toward the bedroom, the phone rang. Initially, he hesitated, not really wanting to talk to anyone about anything; however, this time he felt compelled to pick up the phone. "Hello."

"Julius, this is Brad. Are you watching the news?"

Julius sighed deeply. "No, this has been a really rough couple of days. I need to tell you—"

Before Julius could say another word, Mr. Broussard interrupted, "You've been exonerated, Julius—they are dropping all charges. It's over, man—it's over!"

Julius stood silently. His mouth was wide open, but he could find no words.

"Julius, are you there?"

"Yes, I'm here."

"Look, Julius, you just turn on the news and get you a paper. We will get together later and talk about a lawsuit against those bastards!"

Julius heard words through the phone, but those words had no meaning to him. He muttered an acknowledgment into the phone and gently put it down.

Julius walked into the kitchen and brewed a pot of coffee. He didn't even attempt to turn on the flat-screen that was mounted under the cabinet. He waited patiently as the coffee splattered down into the pot and watched intently as the last few drops fell. Julius poured the coffee into his favorite cup, the one that Tiara had given him on boss's day soon after she had started working for him. Julius stared at the cup as he slowly filled the cup. He inhaled deeply and allowed the aroma of the coffee to completely affect his senses. Julius, with his hot cup of coffee in tow, walked slowly to his media room. He picked up the remote, but before he pressed the power button, he took a few sips of his coffee. He shook his head slowly in pleasurable agreement, as the taste and aroma worked their magic.

Finally, he pointed the remote toward the screen. He quickly found channel eleven, and right on cue, the "BREAKING NEWS" was being broadcast. Julius turned the volume up load and listened intently. "Businessman Julius Dent has been cleared of any involvement in the murder of his wife…" Julius was numb. He didn't really know how to react. This should have been news that made him jump for joy, but instead, he simply sipped from his cup and sat emotionless, staring at the screen.

Finally, after several minutes, Julius turned and pressed the off button on the remote. He went to the utility closet and took out all of his cleaning supplies and started cleaning. From his master bath to the garage, Julius wiped, scrubbed, swept, and mopped until he could do no more. Julius wiped the sweat from his brow and sighed. He didn't know whether to laugh or cry; his emotions were lost somewhere in between anger and sadness.

"Now what?" Julius plopped down in the deep leather recliner. He looked around the room at all the designer furniture, art pieces, and plush rugs. "I would give it all up just to have one more moment with you." With those words Julius got up and walked toward the bathroom to take a long, hot shower. He stood and allowed the hot water to run over his head. It seemed to clear his mind. He found himself thinking of what he needed to do to get back on track. He had pretty much given his managers the responsibility of running his business and left the money management to his accountants, but he knew that he needed to thrust himself back into his business, and if nothing else, to drown himself with his work as a distraction from his pain.

Julius moaned as the steady hot stream pulsated against his neck, shoulders, and back. His muscles ached as if he had just finished a long grueling workout. Julius realized how much had happened in the past forty-eight hours. He was amazed at how quickly things had happened and even more amazed at his sudden change of fate. Then it hit him—he realized that Pam must have made calls to initiate clearing his name. Julius turned off the shower, grabbed a towel, and slowly dried himself off. "I need to call and apologize for leaving the way that I did." Julius walked into the bedroom, picked up the phone, and sat down on the end of the bed. "Damn, I don't know the number." Then he remembered that he had her number on his cell phone. Julius found his cell and quickly found Pam's number.

"Hello."

Julius was startled to hear a man's voice. "Sorry, I must have the wrong…"

"Are you looking for Pam Cooper?"

"Yes, this is Julius Dent." The man quickly identified himself as John Franks. "I don't think that we have officially met, Mr. Dent; I'm the Assistant DA. Pam has told me everything, and I am so very sorry for all that has happened. I just want you to know that I'm the one who was responsible for missing evidence and information on this case. It was my fault, Mr. Dent, and—"

Julius stopped John in mid-sentence. "Look, Mr. Franks, none of that matters right now. It can't be changed, and none of this will bring my wife back to me. I realize that you two were trying to do your job."

"I just wanted you to know that I was the one that was responsible for preparing the case—Pam was merely presenting the evidence that I provided her. I failed her, and frankly, you as well."

Julius thanked John for his acknowledgment of fault and asked,

"How is Pam?"

"The doctor just left. Pam was very lucky. It was a nasty wound, but no vital organs were damaged. She just lost a lot of blood. They are going to watch her today and probably release her tomorrow. Would you like to speak to her?"

"Yes," Julius replied unhesitatingly. John handed Pam the phone and walked out of the room. He knew that Pam would want the opportunity to speak with Julius from the heart.

"Julius, I—"

"Wait, Pam, let me apologize for leaving the way that I did. I was about to have a moment, and I didn't want for you to see me emotional."

"Mr. Dent, I fully understand you being emotional. What we put you through must have been unbearable. I just want you to know that I won't rest until we have completely..."

"Pam, it's done—all day, I've had time to think about this whole mess. My wife is dead, but her spirit will live on in my heart forever. You took a chance because you doubted whether I killed my wife. If you hadn't, I would be destined to live the rest of my life incarcerated and Denise..." Julius paused. He thought of how tragic this whole situation had been, of how Denise, who he had really genuinely cared for, was dead.

Thoughts ran through his mind of how he would never know why the person who he had shared so much with, both professionally and personally, had betrayed him. He couldn't understand how a person who seemed so very loyal and loving to both he and Tiara, could turn so quickly to become a—well—a murderer. "Pam, I just wanted to let you know that I don't blame you; how could I—you almost died taking a chance on my innocence. I just wanted to call and let you know that in my heart, I know what type of person you are, and I will not forget that. For now, just get better. We will sit down and talk about all of this once everything settles down."

"Thank you, Julius, thank you." Pam took a deep breath and smiled. She realized that after all that he had been through, Julius still did not seem vengeful. She knew in her heart that he was a genuine, good man.

Chapter 16

Julius drove toward his office on Peachtree. He pulled up into the parking lot across from the building and stared at the long dark windows. He marveled at the reflection of the clouds floating aimlessly across the face of the building. He smiled, got out of the car, and walked confidently toward the double doors with the marquee of Dent Enterprises proudly displayed. Julius punched in his security code and listened for the familiar chirp as the locks released and granted him entry. Julius pushed open the doors, walked in, stood, and stared. He turned 360 degrees and marveled that the office was neat and orderly. Julius walked through the main office area, down the hall, and into his office. He looked around his office and smiled as evidence of Tiara's decorative prowess enticed him. He sat down behind his desk. He ran his hand up and down the arms of his deep plush chair, enjoying the feel of the soft cool leather.

There were two neatly stacked bundles of mail on his desk with a sheet of paper on each. The one to the left was marked "PERSONAL," the other, "BUSINESS." As Julius reached toward the stack of business mail, he thought aloud, "I know Tiara. I need to take the time for the personal things in life before I engulf myself in the business." Julius smiled as he grabbed the stack of personal mail. As he scanned through the stack, tears filled his eyes as he read line after line, card after card, of words of encouragement. He marveled at how many people were supporting him and did not believe that he would ever have harmed his wife.

Julius reached for a card in a black envelope with gold script typing. Julius hesitated. "Wonder who this one is from?" As Julius picked up the card, the scent of Denise's perform hit him a like a brick. His hands started to tremble as he slowly opened the envelope. He pulled the card from the envelope. The front of the card read, "IN TIMES LIKE THESE." Julius opened the card, "TRUST IN…," the name "GOD" had been scratched through and the word "ME" and been handwritten in big bold letters. It was signed, Denise. At the bottom of the card was "P.S.—LOVE TO DEATH."

Julius shook his head from side to side. He simply could not understand why. "This is some senseless bullshit!" Julius grabbed all of the cards and letters and placed them in the bottom drawer of his desk. He sat back in his chair and stared at the stack of business mail. "No, not today." Julius got up and walked out of the office. As he walked toward the front door, he noticed a news truck parked in front. The crew hadn't quite set up yet, but it was obvious that they were about to do a story using his office as a backdrop.

"Damn the luck!" At first Julius started to wait them out, going back into his office until they finished, but instead, he decided to take advantage of them not being set up and get the hell out of there. Julius knew that he would have to face the media soon, but just not now. He opened the door, quickly punched in his security code and walked quickly toward his car.

At first, the people talking beside the van seemed oblivious to him, but as he got closer, the reporter stared right at him and yelled, "Mr. Dent!" Julius realized that the camera was not even out of the van yet and the anchor did not have a microphone.

He stopped, the crew sprang into action, but Julius knew that they were going to lose this opportunity. "Mr. Dent, can we please have an interview?"

Julius looked into the eyes of the reporter and asked, "What's your name?"

"Cynthia LaMay," the reporter blurted.

"Well, Ms. LaMay, I'll make a deal with you; if you tell your crew to wait until I'm gone before you do your story, I promise that I will give you my first interview."

Cynthia looked into Julius's eyes; she had never personally met him, but knew instantly that he meant exactly what he was saying. She signaled for her crew to stop and walked closer to Julius. She motioned for him to walk on toward his car. As they walked she whispered, "Mr. Dent, we were just doing our jobs."

Julius stopped, reached out his hand to the young lady. "First of all, call me Julius…"

His firm but gentle handshake caught Cynthia off guard; this was not what she had expected. She swallowed hard, and was barely able to say, "OK—Julius."

"Secondly, I will let you know how I feel about that when you get your interview." Cynthia almost reluctantly released Julius's hand as he got into his car and slowly drove away. Julius smiled as he looked in his rear-view mirror, "Still got it, boy—still got it!"

Cynthia turned and walked back toward her news crew. She tried to regain her composure, but was obviously affected by her short conversation with Julius. She stopped dead in her tracks, "Shit, I didn't give him my card!" Second-guessing her decision not to press Julius for an interview, Cynthia turned around quickly and cursed loudly as Julius's car slowly faded from sight. "I certainly hope he keeps his word," she mumbled to herself as she and her crew walked toward the front door of Dent Enterprises and began shooting their news story. After several minutes, they wrapped up the shoot, gathered their equipment and walked back toward the van. Caught up in conversation with her crew, Cynthia had not noticed that Julius had returned and parked his car directly behind the news van.

Julius lightly tapped his horn—in unison, the crew looked. Julius motioned for Cynthia. As she walked toward him, Julius smiled as he noticed the extra little push that she was giving to her hips, accentuating her curvaceous figure. Although she was dressed very conservatively, Julius could certainly see that not only was Cynthia very attractive, she was sexy as hell! Julius tried his best to keep eye contact; he did not want to make that type of impression so quickly. As she walked up to the car, Julius professionally stated, "I'll need your card so I can contact you for that interview."

Cynthia smiled at Julius, and like a magician that had practiced her trick thousands of times, handed him her business card. This time though, she was prepared. "Wait, let me give you my cell number as well, just in case…"

"In case what?" Julius interjected.

"In case you can't reach me at work." Without another word, Cynthia turned and walked away. She didn't have to turn around to look—she knew that Julius would be carefully studying her movements—of course, she was right. Julius's eyes were fixed on the sensual swaying of her hip. The almost hypnotic motion startled him, as did the swelling sensation pushing hard against his jeans. "Calm down," Julius whispered to himself. "How can I even think like this…?" Julius paused as he realized that it had been over eighteen months since Tiara had died. He did a quick emotion check and realized that for the first time, he didn't feel guilt when looking at another woman sexually. He now knew that he was emotionally ready to explore, but he knew that he had to be careful; he certainly did not want to get involved with any psychos again—no, never again.

Chapter 17

Pam stared in the mirror at the row of neatly arranged stitches on her right side just below her rib cage. She lightly ran her fingers across each stitch, awestruck at the neat and tightly sewn wound. She couldn't believe, but was certainly thankful that the knife had missed all of her vital organs, and as the doctor had explained, although it was a gusher, no serious internal damage had been done. She recalled the searing pain as Denise had thrust the knife in her. She remembered feeling as if she were falling in slow motion as Julius ran frantically toward her. She smiled and found it strange that she would remember that Julius smelled as if he had just walked out of the shower as he pressed against her side, trying to stop the bleeding. She didn't see it, but vividly remember the loud gunshot, then—nothing. Her next memory was of lying in the hospital bed, with Julius looking down into her eyes. Pam knew that she was lucky to be alive and that she had Julius to thank for that.

Pam walked to her study and stared at the shelves of books and all of the plaques, awards, and certificates sprawled neatly across the walls. She wondered if it was all worth it and wondered if maybe this wasn't for her anymore. Pam sat behind her desk and lamented over all that had happened during the past eighteen months. She leaned forward and cringed as she inadvertently put too much pressure on her wound. She held her breath and closed her eyes tightly as she felt the urge to get emotional.

"I've got to get ahold of this. What happened—happened; now I have to get my mind back in the right place." Pam leaned back in her chair and took some long, slow, deep breaths. Once again she went through the same ritual that she had gone through thousands of times before to help her relax. As she tensed her muscles, she felt but ignored the pain in her side, and as her mind let go, the pain melted away. Pam slowly opened her eyes as she pushed the last bit of air from her lungs. She looked around her study again, but this time saw all that she had worked so hard for, and all she had left to do.

Pam got up and walked toward her bedroom, and was startled as the doorbell chimed loudly. "Who in the world could that be?" Pam knew that it wouldn't be John, because he had dropped her off only an hour ago and thought that she would be resting. She walked to the front door and peeked through the peephole. It was someone delivering flowers. Somewhat cautious, Pam pressed her intercom button and asked, "Can I help you?"

The voice responded, "Delivery for Ms. Cooper." Pam opened the door. The young man handed Pam a beautiful arrangement of white roses. Pam thanked him and was about to close the door. "Wait, there's more." He walked back toward his van and started setting out vase after vase full of different colored roses—ten dozen to be exact. Pam stood there with her mouth literally wide open. The last arrangement brought in had a card attached. Pam waited until the van had pulled away, then turned and looked. "Well, I guess I know who did this." She walked over and pulled the card from the arrangement, "No, I want to savor this moment."

Pam put the card in her robe pocket and walked toward the kitchen. She put on a pot of coffee, sat, and waited patiently. Pam was almost giddy with anticipation as she slowly filled her cup. She walked over, sat at the table and sat the card down beside the cup. Initially, she reached for the card, but grabbed the cup instead. She blew gently into the coffee then sipped. Pam nodded her head slowly as the combination of taste and aroma worked its magic.

She picked the card up and thought to herself, "Why am I getting all worked up about this—I know that these are from Julius, and he probably just called and asked for these to be delivered—with some standard thank you card." Convinced that she was getting excited for nothing, she started to open the card, but as she brought the card closer, a familiar scent permeated her nostrils—it was Julius's cologne. Pam's eyes widened and her heartbeat increased as she read the small card, "The first time I looked into your eyes, I saw your heart....Julius." The card grew blurry, as tears quickly filled Pam's eyes. She again started to realize how enormous a mistake she had made and how tragic this whole situation was. Pam sobbed openly, finally allowing herself to release the emotions that her professional life dictated stay hidden safely away.

After a couple minutes, Pam wiped her tears away with the sleeve of her robe. "I guess I needed that." Pam wondered whether Julius's gesture was intended to be romantic, or just him being grateful. "Well, whatever—I will just enjoy the fantasy; whatever will be—will be." Pam turned her attention back to her coffee and slowly sipped her concerns away.

Pam finished her coffee, got up and walked toward her bedroom. As she passed a vase of pink roses, she leaned forward and inhaled deeply. "Mr. Dent, this is the last thing that I want to think about before I go to sleep. Maybe you will come to me in my dreams." Pam grabbed the vase and took it with her to the bedroom. As she sat the vase down on her bedside table, she noticed that her cell phone message light was blinking. "I wonder who that could be. I didn't hear it ring." Pam quickly remembered that John had put her phone on vibrate while they were at the hospital. She picked up her phone and saw that there were a lot of missed calls showing—two from John, three from her office, and two from a number that she did not recognize. Feeling somewhat tired, Pam decided not to bother with the messages, so she turned her cell phone off and turned the ringer off on her home phone so that she would not be disturbed from her much-needed rest.

Pam gently lay down, her head sinking deep into her pillow. She was pleasantly surprised that she was in no pain at all. As she lay there, her eyes focused on the little diamond sitting proudly surrounded by a small cluster of gold. She waited impatiently for thoughts and memories of her Granny to fill her with inspiration and hope, but frustratingly, those thoughts and memories would not come. Unnerved at her mind's failure, she turned and looked toward the vase of pink roses. She marveled at their near perfection and how quickly the sweet aroma permeated her senses. She closed her eyes and allowed herself to bask in a fantastical moment of pleasure; that lasted until she fell into a deep, peaceful sleep.

Chapter 18

Brenda lay in bed staring intently at the tiny light on the smoke detector that would blink every thirty seconds. She waited patiently for the nurses to make their rounds and prepared herself to put on her show—the show that she had concocted with the help of her big sister when she first came here as a little girl, and had since mastered. Brenda knew that since she had turned eighteen the previous week, they really couldn't prevent her from leaving, unless they could determine that she was a threat to herself or others. She and Denise had gone over this time and time again; she knew that she was prepared. Denise had taught her well, and she had all the knowledge that any eighteen-year-old should have; she just wondered whether the time was right for her to stop the show or if she needed to plan more carefully what she intended to do when she got out.

Like clockwork, the door to her room slowly pushed open and one of her nurses strode in. Without speaking she handed Brenda a cup with two pills and held another with water in her hands. Brenda sat up in her bed and stared at the tiny cup in her hand. She looked up at the nurse and for the first time in nine years said, "I don't think that I will be needing those any longer."

Completely caught off guard, the nurse dropped the cup of water, turned, and ran almost frantically from the room. In seconds, she returned with the charge nurse. "Brenda, did you say something?"

Brenda stared at the both of them and wondered whether she should not say another word, but sensing that the time had come, she said, "Yes, I did." Both nurses stood there, with their mouths open wide. They were taken completely off guard. "You stay here, I will call Dr. Jamison; she simply won't believe this." The charge nurse ran from the room as the other stared in wonderment.

"Honey, how are you doing?"

Brenda had direct eye contact with the nurse, something that she never did before. "I'm a little sad because my big sister hasn't come to visit me in a while."

Thinking that Brenda did not know that her sister was dead, the nurse said, "I'm sure that your sister will visit you soon." Brenda bit down on her lip to calm herself. She could tell by the look on the nurse's face that she knew that her sister was dead, and she also knew that Dr. Jamison would be the one to break that type of news to her. Brenda didn't want to give them the idea that she already knew about what happened to her sister. She needed to give the impression that when they did tell her, she was able to accept it, deal with it, and move on. Brenda knew that this would be much more difficult than what she had done over the past nine years because her sister was all that she had left in the world. She wasn't sure if she could contain the rage that had built in her mind long enough to get through what she knew would be a thorough mental status evaluation.

Dr. Jamison walked into the room and motioned for the nurse to leave. She pulled up a chair and sat directly in front of Brenda. "Hello, sweetie, do you know who I am?" Brenda nodded yes, but did not speak. "They tell me that you have been talking." Brenda looked at her and smiled. Dr. Jamison's head cocked to one side. This was the first time that Brenda had looked directly in her eyes. She was almost amazed at the glow in her light brown eyes and was astonished that she had not realized that she had watched a little nine-year-old girl grow into—well—a beautiful young lady.

"Dr. Jamison, I'm doing just fine, but I do miss my sister."

Dr. Jamison's eyes filled with tears. This was the first time in nine years that she had actually heard Brenda's soft, gentle voice. Dr. Jamison took a long, deep breath, "Well, it's so nice to finally get a chance to hear you. Do you remember anything about what we have talked about?"

Brenda paused, "Well, I may not remember everything, but I do know that you talk too much sometimes."

Dr. Jamison chuckled aloud, marveling at how crisp and clean Brenda spoke, and how her thought process seemed to be intact. "Why didn't you talk to us?"

Brenda took her time and thought hard about the countless hours that she and her sister had spent whispering to each other, the countless hours of silence that she had to endure alone, the countless sleepless nights, the countless nightmares and horror of remembering. Her eyes filled with tears. "I wanted to, but every time that I would think about saying something, I would see my dad sitting next to me, bleeding, dying, and asking me why; I would see my mother sitting in her car, bleeding, dying, and asking me why...I didn't know why, so what was I supposed to say?"

Dr. Jamison leaned toward Brenda. "I suppose that you should say whatever is on your mind—and remember, you can always tell me whatever—"

Brenda interrupted, "Can I go home now?"

Caught off guard, Dr. Jamison stammered, "Well, see—if...when—we will talk about that just a little bit later—OK?" Somewhat disappointed, Brenda nodded in agreement.

From the corner of her eye, Dr. Jamison could see the nurses standing in the hallway, close to the door, obviously just as interested in hearing what Brenda had to say. "Excuse me for a minute." Dr. Jamison pushed her chair away from the bed and walked to the door. She whispered to the nurses, "You can read my report later; for now we need privacy." She closed the door and walked back over to Brenda.

Thoughts were racing through Brenda's mind. She really didn't know how much she should talk, how much she should tell—then she remembered what Dee Dee had told her: "You will know when the time is right—but only tell them enough to get what you want; never tell them everything."

Dr. Jamison sat back down in the chair next to Brenda, "It was not your—"

Brenda, sensing that she needed to think more before she continued, blurted, "I'm tired now. I think I need to rest."

Disappointed, Dr. Jamison smiled. "All right, I will come back to see you after lunch."

Brenda gave her a big smile, and on cue let out a big yawn. Dr. Jamison turned and walked out of the room.

Brenda sighed loudly. It was refreshing to her not to have to hide that she was able to speak and to show them that she was not stupid. Brenda knew that some of the nurses would be wondering if she remembered some of the horrible comments they had made about her, and some of the nasty things that she had allowed them to do...things that she had not told her big sister about; but there were also other things that she hadn't told her sister about, things that kept gnawing at her mind, things that kept her from sleeping at night. Brenda knew that she needed some time to think, time to sort out some things before she put her final plans into action. She already had her list of who had hurt her—taken advantage of her youthful innocence—and she knew exactly what fate they would have when the time was right.

Brenda closed her eyes and brought back the memory of when her father died. She remembered hearing Dee Dee screaming and remembered opening the door to see her father hitting her big sister. She remembered how angry she felt seeing her father slam his fist hard against her sister's face, and how helpless she felt knowing that there was nothing that she could do to help. She remembered how angrily her father had glared at her when he saw her standing in the doorway and remembered how her big sister had tried to save her by attempting to stab him with the letter opener. She also remembered that her father had turned back toward Denise as she was thrusting the letter opener toward him. She remembered seeing her father moving slightly out of the way just in time, and that the letter opener only cut him on his neck. She remembered her father hitting Denise so violently that she just crumpled to the floor and remembered her father kneeling over her with his hands wrapped tightly around her neck, choking the life from her.

She remembered how cold the letter opener felt in her hand as she ran up behind her father, and how easily it pushed through his flesh when she thrust it deep into his neck. She thought of how she had wanted for so many years to tell her sister that she was the one who actually killed their father, but that she was afraid that it would make them grow apart.

She needed desperately to tell her that for the past three years, like clockwork, fifteen minutes after the nurses thought that she had taken her nighttime medication, they would come back as she pretended to be asleep, fondle and kiss her. She had kept her promise to her big sister; she did not say a word to anyone but her, but she had suffered immeasurable pain and humiliation in almost total solitude. She had endured; now it was time for her to avenge. Her mind was conditioned, and she felt that she owed it to her sister. "Don't worry, Dee Dee," Brenda mumbled. "They will pay—all of them will pay!"

Brenda allowed herself to sleep. She was no longer afraid of the thoughts of terror and pain. In fact, she invited them—she now knew that she was ready.

Chapter 19

Julius looked at himself in his rearview mirror. This was his first day back to his office in some time, and he wanted to make sure that he at least looked ready. He brushed down his thin mustache with his fingers. "Back to the grind." Julius knew that this was basically the first day of the rest of his life. He no longer had to walk around and wonder what people were thinking of him, or what he may have done to his wife. Julius straightened his tie, got out of his car, and walked briskly to the front of the building. He paused for a minute to look at the marquee painted neatly on the glass doors. "Here we go." Julius took a long, deep breath, held it for a moment, and then slowly let it out as he walked through the door.

As he walked in a thunderous roar and applause erupted. All of his office workers, restaurant managers, and some of his business associates had gathered to welcome him back. Julius stood there, looking at all of the people that had come. He made eye contact with his secretary, Carolyn. He shook his finger at her as she hunched her shoulders, playing "Ms. Innocent." He knew that she was the only one that knew that he was coming back to work this morning, and obviously she had set him up. Carolyn ran over and gave Julius a big hug. "Welcome back, Julius," she whispered in his ear.

Julius smiled, kissed her on the cheek, and whispered, "You know you are in trouble."

Carolyn stood back, put her hands on her hips. "And?"

Julius shook his head as the crowd burst out in laughter. As much as Julius hated to admit it, this was exactly what he needed. He had dreaded the thought of having to run into his business associates and friends one-by-one and having to tell the same story over and over again of all that had happened. He knew that everyone would be curious, especially since only sketchy details were released in the news.

Julius was delighted as he shook hands and exchanged pleasantries with everyone. He didn't have to walk around much because each person seemingly was drawn to him like a magnet; he certainly hadn't lost his ability to captivate. After about thirty minutes, Julius climbed on top of his receptionist's desk. "I would like to thank all of you for coming. You all have no idea how very much this means to me. I just want you to know that I…" Julius paused and looked down. He fought hard to hold back the tears.

Then someone yelled out, "We love you, man!"

Julius smiled, climbed down from the desk, and waved to everyone as he disappeared down the hallway and into his office.

Julius looked around his office. He could tell that Carolyn had been busy. Everything had been perfectly organized. She had done a great job at taking care of him through all of this. He knew that she had to be overwhelmed, because she had been taking care of her normal duties, plus she was handling everything that a personal assistant should do. She had filled his daily calendar with things that needed to be done now, highlighted in red, and things that would need attention within a week or so, highlighted in yellow. She had separated his messages into two categories: important and not so important. Julius smiled; he knew that she was trying to make his return to work as simple as possible.

Julius's thoughts were interrupted by a knock on his office door. Carolyn stuck her head through the door. "Are you ready?" Julius looked puzzled. Carolyn again put her hands on her hips and stared menacingly at Julius. He looked down on his planner and the first highlighted in red was a 10:00 a.m. meeting with his staff. Julius shook his head, realizing that it was time to get back to business. Julius got up and walked toward the conference room. As he walked in, he could see that no one had forgotten how he was about meetings. Everyone was quiet and ready to take notes. Julius had always insisted that his office be a happy and fun place to work, but he had also demanded professionalism when it came time to get down to business; everyone knew that it was time to get down to business.

At the head of the table, where Julius sat, were four file folders: three bearing the name of one of his restaurants, the fourth labeled office. Julius opened one file folder at a time. He punched numbers in his calculator and wrote down notes as he studied the content of each folder. Julius put the pen down and sighed loudly. He looked around the room slowly at each person. Julius did not speak for, to them, what seemed like minutes. "I'm going to need a new receptionist and a new secretary."

Carolyn's mouth dropped as everyone stared at each other in stark surprise. The receptionist was the only person not in the room because she was manning the phones. "Someone get Sue." Carolyn, now almost in tears, left hurriedly and returned within seconds. "Sue, you are my new secretary. Carolyn, you are my personal assistant."

The room burst out in laughter as the look on Carolyn's and Sue's faces turned from terror to delight. "All right," Julius interrupted. "Actually, I am offering you two these positions, but only if you want them." In unison, Carolyn and Sue accepted Julius's offer.

Julius regained control over the now rumbling group. "OK, people, let's get through this. We have a business to run." Julius's face grew stern so everyone knew what was coming; at least they thought they knew. "I've looked at our numbers. All of you know how I am about this business. I expect each and every one of you to treat this business as if it were your own. We are here not only to make money, but to keep our clientele happy. Without a commitment to excellence, we cannot achieve either. When I put someone in a position of authority, I expect for them to handle-up. I cannot and will not tolerate sub-par performance or attitude."

Julius's brow rose as he stared around the room. He certainly had everyone's undivided attention. "All of you know what I have been going through for the past, well, almost two years, and I appreciate all that you have done to support me, but what you have done to my business—well..." Everyone in the room was on edge. "Well, all I can say is that every single person in this room will...get a big-ass raise—because under the circumstances, you have done a wonderful job!" Julius got up, walked around and shook every single individual's hand. He was really appreciative of his team; they proved that they truly had his back.

Julius walked back to the front of the room. "All of you have proven that you are trustworthy and dependable, and I thank each of you....now, let's go make some money!" There was not a single person in the room that wasn't touched by the strength that Julius was showing. They were proud of themselves for believing and trusting a man who they knew wasn't capable of killing, especially someone for whom he obviously had an undying love. Everyone left the room except Carolyn and Sue. It was if they knew that Julius would need to talk to them privately; he did.

Julius shook his head and smiled. "Have a seat. Both of you know what I have been through. I trusted Denise with my life—and because of that, Tiara is dead. It is extremely important for me to know that I won't have to worry, ever again, about…"

Carolyn, tears streaming down her face, interrupted Julius, "If we had any idea that Denise felt that way about you, we would have told you. Ever since we found out that it was her, we have talked and talked, asking everyone if they had noticed any signs—Julius, no one knew; she was obviously sick. You will never have to worry about us." Sue nodded in agreement.

"Well, I know that I put you two on the spot offering you new positions. Are you sure that you want them?"

Carolyn and Sue looked at each other simultaneously and burst out into laughter. Grinning ear-to-ear Carolyn anxiously answered, "Yes, Mr. Dent—and we are ready to get started." As they were leaving the room, Julius asked, "Sue…"

"Don't worry, Mr. Dent; I can handle both until we get a chance to hire a new receptionist." Sue quickly put Julius's mind to rest with her reassurance.

Julius just shook his head. His people knew him like a book, and he knew that this was why they never believed that he would or could kill his wife. "I'm depending on the both of you to help me get back on track. I'm not sure when I will be ready to interview any new people, so…."

"Julius," Carolyn interjected. "We wouldn't know who to trust right now anyway." Julius smiled as the ladies turned and left the room.

Julius walked back to his office and sat down behind his desk. He turned around in his chair so that it was facing the window. He stared and marveled at how magnificently blue the sky was and how the clouds' imperfect shapes were seemingly perfect in every way. He smiled as he thought that he had never taken the time to see the beauty in the sky until he met Tiara. He turned back around and looked at the picture of him and Tiara on his desk. He knew that he had lost his lover and best friend and that there would never be anyone to take her place, but he also knew that he had always loved the attention that only a woman could give, and he certainly loved giving it back.

Julius closed his eyes, took a long, deep breath, and held it. As he exhaled, in his mind he released. Julius picked up the picture of him and his wife, walked over, and put it on the bookshelf. He traced his finger around the image of Tiara. "OK, babe, I'm ready." With that, Julius walked back to his desk, sat down, and started calling all of his business associates, one-by-one. As he spoke to each, he thanked them for standing by his side and assured them that their loyalty would never be forgotten.

Julius was on the phone for three straight hours, relentlessly calling to make sure that he did not miss one person. When he finally finished, he noticed that it was already 5:30 p.m. Julius got up and stretched. His neck and shoulders were stiff, and for the first time since he could remember, his mind was tired from something other than worrying about the murder of his wife. Julius grabbed his keys and walked out the door. As he walked toward the front, he noticed that Carolyn and Sue were still there, moving some of their things from office to office and desk to desk. Without saying a word, Julius put his keys in his pocket and helped the ladies finish moving. After about thirty minutes or so, Julius was carrying the last few items that Carolyn needed for her office. Julius noticed some boxes on the floor just outside the office doors. Julius bent down to bring them in.

"No, Julius, those are some of Denise's personal items. I will take care of them tomorrow." All of a sudden a rush of sadness came over him. Although Denise had killed his wife and tried to kill Pam, he still felt compassion. Noticing the sudden change in his demeanor, Carolyn and Sue each grabbed Julius by the hand. "It's been a long day, Julius—let's get out of here."

Julius nodded in agreement as they left the office. Julius turned to punch in the security code on the door, and noticed that Sue was standing with her hands on her hips and tapping her foot. Julius laughed loudly and moved aside as Sue stepped up and punched in the security code. They all burst out in laughter as Sue "popped her neck" from side to side. "Well, I am the new secretary!" They all laughed as Julius escorted them to their cars.

Julius smiled. "You two be careful…see you tomorrow." Julius hit the auto-start button on his key remote and walked toward his car. Julius sat in his car for a moment listening to the gentle, muffled sound of his engine. He pressed the gas pedal slightly and smiled as his engine responded with a gentle growl. "That's my girl." He put the car in gear, but before he could drive off, he felt his cell phone vibrating. He looked down to see that it was Carolyn.

"Hello…"

"I just called Body Worx. They are waiting on you."

"For that, my friend, you get the bonus prize!" Julius thanked Carolyn and sped off toward the spa. Although he was tired, he knew that this was exactly—well, maybe not exactly—but he needed a massage; yes, he definitely needed a massage.

Julius parked in front of Body Worx. He remembered the first time he and Tiara had come here for a massage and how wonderful an experience it had been. As he walked through the doors, he was pleasantly greeted. "Hello, Mr. Dent, we are so happy to see you again." Julius could tell that they had made some special preparations and, almost embarrassed by this special attention, he humbly acknowledged everyone as three wonderfully pleasant ladies escorted him to his changing and shower room.

As the ladies left, Julius quickly discarded his clothing and stepped into the shower. Julius sighed deeply as the hot water pulsated down on his tense shoulders and neck. Normally, he would have stayed in the shower for at least fifteen minutes, but he was anticipating his massage, so after about five minutes, he was draped in his robe and walking through the doors to the massage room.

Julius knew the routine all too well, as he disrobed and climbed onto the warmed massage bed. The ambience of the room was perfect. The lighting was dimmed, soothing music played, and mildly scented candles filled the air. "Hello, Mr. Dent." Renee, Julius's favorite masseuse, walked over to him. "We have been so very worried about—"

Julius stopped her in mid-sentence. "Its OK, I'm just happy that it's over. I'm ready to get on with my life…starting with this." Renee smiled and started her massage. There was a reason that Renee was Julius's favorite masseuse, and she was thoroughly reminding him of it. Tiara would always tease him by asking did he get a hard on when she would massage him and he would always respond—"Hell yea!" Well, that was an inside joke, because Renee was the consummate professional. Mastery of her work had always been her objective, and it showed. This time was no different; after about thirty minutes, Julius was totally relaxed.

Renee, sensing that she had accomplished her goal, grabbed a warm sheet, covered Julius, and quietly left the room. Julius lay there for another thirty minutes, before he finally got up. As always, Renee had his clothes neatly arranged and ready. As Julius was putting on his clothes, he noticed that Renee had placed a business card in one of his shoes. On the back of the card, Renee had written a phone number and the word, "Anytime!" It was quite obvious to Julius, now that the word was out that he was cleared of any involvement in his wife's murder, this would be the norm. Julius sat and thought for a moment. It just didn't feel quite right yet, but he couldn't deny the warm feeling such attention gave him. Julius put the card in his pocket, finished dressing, and left the spa. He just wanted to go home and continue to enjoy his relaxed state of mind.

Chapter 20

Judge Jones stared across the table at Pam and John as he finished reading the report that they had painstakingly prepared. Although it had been almost four months since the State had dropped the charges against Julius, the judge was still bitter.

"Ms. Cooper, my first thought is to sanction you. It appears that you could be in violation of client-attorney privilege by meeting with Mr. Dent without his attorney present…however, I have already spoken to Mr. Broussard, and he has indicated that when you became aware of certain errors, you did in fact contact him with the information. Since you had the best interest of justice in mind, I will take no punitive actions against you."

Pam showed no emotion, she simply acknowledged the judge with a quaint nod. The judge looked at John and motioned for him to leave the room. Pam took a deep breath. She knew that she was about to get a lecture from a man who had discretely mentored her over the past ten years.

"Pam, I've been doing this for over thirty years. When you first came to my courtroom as a young assistant DA, I told you that if you worked hard and studied your craft, you had the potential to be great. You made serious mistakes on this case, but I'm smart enough to realize that the mistake that you made was giving someone else too much autonomy. I just want you to know that I'm angry not that you made mistakes, but that you put yourself in harm's way." Pam's eyes filled with tears. "You came very close to losing your life and I don't care how much passion you have for your job, or how much you wanted to correct a wrong, you simply cannot put your life in danger." Judge Jones pushed a box of tissues close to Pam. "Now, this is over and we will not revisit it again—in the future, make sure that your people are ready before you give them too much rope."

Pam looked up at Judge Jones. "Thank you." As Pam was about to leave, she turned back to the judge. "I could see it in his eyes…" Then she turned to walk out.

Judge Jones shook his head. He could tell by her reaction that she had developed some type of feelings for Julius. "You be careful; you may not be so lucky again."

Pam knew that he could see right through her, so she did not pretend. "I'm a big girl." She smiled and walked out of the room. As Pam walked toward John, who had been waiting in the lobby area, thoughts of Julius ran through her mind. "Why do I even expect for him to call me? I should really just stop; I have too much else to worry about." In her mind, Pam tried hard to convince herself that it was just a weird chain of tragic events that brought them together, and that she should expect nothing more.

John could see that Pam had been crying. "Are you OK?"

Pam nodded yes as they walked down the long hallway toward their own office. When they walked through the doors of the office, Pam was met by her secretary, Mae, with a handful of messages and a basket full of cases to review. John reached for the cases.

"No, I want to review them first." John turned red with embarrassment. He was somewhat surprised since this was the first time that Pam had reacted this way. "John, I want you to work on the Delgado case." John looked at Pam in total shock. The Delgado case was another big case, one that would take their best effort to win.

"Close your mouth, you may catch a fly—you will not make another mistake."

John loosened the knot of his tie. "You know that I won't." John quickly walked away, ecstatic to know that Pam had not lost faith in his ability to do a good job.

As Pam turned to walk into her office, Mae handed her a handwritten note. "I thought that maybe I should wait to give you this." Puzzled, Pam took the note from Mae's hand; it was from Julius. "He came by while you were in the meeting with Judge Jones." Pam tried her best not show what she was feeling, but her heart was racing, and she could tell that she would not be able to fool another woman, so she quickly walked into her office and gently closed the door behind her. She leaned against the door, almost weak from the sudden feeling of excitement. Her hands trembled lightly as she slowly read the message.

"Ms. Cooper, I am sorry that I haven't contacted you in the past few months. I have been so very busy trying to get back in the middle of my business operations and of course busy trying to get a grip on all that has happened. Anyway, sorry I missed you—I wanted to thank you again for everything." The note was signed— Julius. Pam walked over and sat down behind her desk. She hated to admit it, but it was quite obvious by the way she was reacting that she had developed some type of feelings for Julius, she just couldn't figure exactly what she was feeling.

Pam looked down at the calendar on her desk; she had written Julius's cell phone number on the back of one of her business cards and stuck it under the corner of the calendar. She had picked up her phone a thousand times to call him, and a thousand times she had stopped before she could dial the last digit. "What I am I thinking? I really should be ashamed of myself—I'm acting like a teenager... let me go on and call this man." Once again Pam picked up the phone, but this time she did not hesitate; she completed the call.

* * *

Julius sat in the airport chair staring at the men busy loading and performing maintenance checks on the huge aircraft. This was his first business trip in some time. He was looking forward to getting away from Atlanta, even if it was to reconnect with some business associates that he had neglected for almost two years now. Everyone had been so very supportive, he felt obligated to personally meet with each of them rather than send his managers.

Julius felt the familiar vibration of his cell phone on his hip. "Hello."

"Julius, this is Pam Cooper."

Julius's eyes brightened. "Ms. Cooper, I guess you got my little note."

"Yes, I'm very sorry I missed you. I was in a meeting."

"Yes, your secretary told me that she didn't know how long you would be. I was on my way to the airport, but wanted to stop in to see you before I left."

Pam's heart sank to her feet. She thought that maybe Julius was moving away. "Oh, are you going on vacation?" Pam held her breath, waiting for his answer.

"No, I have some business meetings over the next two weeks, so I will be traveling here and there."

Pam, feeling much better now, relaxed and enjoyed a long conversation with Julius. They were finding out how very much they had in common. It had been a while since Julius had enjoyed such conversation, especially with someone he found so very intriguing, and likewise, Pam had been so busy making a name for herself, she had not allowed herself to let her guard down and enjoy the taste of prophetic flirtation. Pam didn't understand why she was so willing to allow Julius inside her world, but she certainly was enjoying this short adventure.

"Pam, I'm sorry, but they just called for boarding. Is it OK if I give you a call later tonight?"

"Of course, Mr. Dent, you can call me."

Julius said goodbye and hurried onto the plane. Julius quickly found his seat on the plane. He always felt a little bit guilty flying first class because he had to fly coach before; he had always considered the "first classers" to be uppity. Julius was humble and had always been one who did not flaunt his success, but he also knew that nothing had been given to him on a silver platter. He put his work in; this was part of his reward. He placed his carry-on in the overhead compartment and settled back in the soft leather seat. By the time the rest of the passengers started filing in, Julius had already plugged in his MP3 player and put on his noise-reducing headphones. He put on his dark shades and tried to be as inconspicuous as possible. He knew that people would recognize him especially since there had been so much news coverage over the past several months. He was relieved after the last passenger had passed him by without any obvious whispers or stares.

As the plane finally started taxiing down the runway, Julius took off his shades. He smiled as he noticed a flight attendant walking toward the front of the plane. Out of respect, he took off his headphones as the flight attendant went through her safety routine. Soon after the flight attendant finished, the plane was lifting gracefully into the air. Julius put his headphones back on, closed his eyes and tried to lose himself in his music. As he settled into his groove, thoughts of his conversation with Pam crept into his mind. He wondered whether he should keep her as just a friend or cross over that indelible line. It was hard for him to discern if what he was feeling was a genuine interest in her or simply a reaction to the volatile situation that they were forced to deal with. At this point, it really didn't matter because he knew that he would be eternally intertwined with her one way or the other. Julius's thoughts were interrupted when the flight attendant tapped him gently on the shoulder. He took off his headphones.

"Would you like something to drink?"

Julius responded, "No, but thank you."

The flight attendant handed Julius a business card. "Someone from coach asked me to give that to you; she said that she knows you."

Julius read the name on the card; it was Cynthia LaMay, the news reporter. "Damn, I completely forgot." Julius motioned to the flight attendant. "Please invite the young lady who gave you this card to sit with me for the remainder of the flight." The flight attendant nodded yes, and smiled as she walked through the curtains to coach.

Within a couple of minutes, Cynthia was standing next to Julius's seat. "Mr. Dent, I wasn't trying to bother you. I just recognized you when I walked past, and wanted to say hello."

"No, please—sit with me. I want to apologize; I completely forgot to call you for that interview. You know that I haven't given an interview yet, and I will keep my promise to you."

Cynthia smiled. "Well, don't worry about it. I know that you have probably been busy getting everything back in order."

"Thank you for understanding. I really expected you to be a little upset with me."

"No, I understand what you must be going through. Don't get me wrong, I'm not saying that I know how you feel, but I can imagine what you have had to deal with."

Julius was caught off guard; he hadn't expected her to be so compassionate. Julius reached out to shake her hand. "Thank you, Ms. LaMay. You don't know how much I appreciate your kindness and understanding." Julius couldn't help but notice the warmth and softness of her hand. The soft sent of her perfume was almost hypnotic. Cynthia smiled as she noticed Julius catching a glimpse of her skirt tightly wrapped around her thighs and his embarrassment as he knew that she knew he was looking.

"I'm sorry, it's been a—"

Cynthia interrupted Julius. "Don't apologize. Let me guess—you haven't been with a woman since…" She didn't have to finish her sentence; Julius was already shaking his head no. "Excuse me for a minute. I'll be right back."

Julius cursed himself under his breath. He had not expected to react this way; this was totally out of character for him. Cynthia returned, opened the overhead compartment, and retrieved a blanket.

She sat down, reclined, and spread the blanket over her legs up to her waist. Julius was about to apologize again but stopped as Cynthia grabbed his hand and placed it under the blanket and between her thighs. Cynthia had gone to lavatory and removed her panties. Julius inhaled deeply as his hand explored her soft wet castle of ecstasy. His heart raced as Cynthia turned her face toward him and sensuously licked her lips. She smiled as she looked at the pleats of his pants being stretched out by the growing bulge that beckoned to be released. Julius realized that Cynthia was allowing him to experience a feeling that he had been reluctant to feel, to reopen a chapter of his life that thus far he had been too guarded to open.

* * *

As the pilot announced that the plane was preparing to land, Cynthia turned to Julius. "I don't want an interview with you."

Surprised, Julius asked, "And why not?"

"You have been through enough—you are no freak show, Mr. Dent. You don't owe us anything."

Julius leaned over and kissed her on the cheek. "Thank you."

Cynthia got up and walked back to her seat. She wondered what Julius would think of her now—whether he would think that she was easy and whorish. She knew that she had put herself on a limb, but instinctively, she felt that she had done exactly the right thing. Cynthia sat down and buckled in. She thought of how nervously gentle Julius had been and how excitedly uncomfortable she had made him feel. "There is just something special about him." Cynthia, finally coming down from that short but sweet encounter with Julius, looked out the window and wondered if she should just drop everything and break Julius off a real peace of good loving. She figured that he would be extremely vulnerable and probably could not resist what she had to offer. She knew that she wasn't available now because she was in a relationship, but she also knew that she may have opened the door to future opportunity.

After the plane landed, all of the passengers hastily exited, hurrying through the terminal to the baggage claim area. Julius was standing at the far end of the carousel, waiting for his luggage to pass. He noticed Cynthia walking toward the carousel, with a gentleman that he immediately recognized as being a professional athlete here in Chicago. Julius and Cynthia made eye contact. Embarrassed, she looked away. When they made eye contact again, Julius gave her a reassuring smile that everything was all right. He had already figured out why she had allowed him such a private privilege. He understood that she was willing to give of herself to help him overcome his self-imposed barrier and to let him know that everyone was not out to hurt him. She obviously didn't need him or his money; she was doing just fine.

Julius grabbed his bag from the carousel and walked quickly to pick up his rental car. He was tired and wanted to get to the hotel to get some much needed rest. He knew that he would need it, because he had a full schedule for the next couple of weeks.

After securing his rental, he made his way to the Omni. Julius felt good that he was about to re-engage with his business associates. In order to protect them from becoming implicated in the things that had happened in his personal life, he had pulled himself away from all of his business associates, leaving that portion of his business to his managers. His managers had done an excellent job at keeping his business in the black, but he knew that there was no one that could make his business prosper the way that he could. He was ready to take his business to the next level, and without the unwarranted stigma hanging over his head, he knew that he could push his business revenues into the stratosphere.

Julius had always disliked the traffic woes in Chicago, but he didn't seem to mind so much this time. He felt a certain sense of calm; his mind relaxed, and he was not bothered by the heavy traffic that was now stop-and-go as he neared the central business district. Julius looked at the tall buildings and marveled at the near-perfect architectural marvels surrounding him. He soaked in the wonderful feeling of his mind being free of all the turmoil that had surrounding him for almost two years. Amazingly, Julius also felt thankful that Cynthia had subtly re-introduced him to pleasures that he had denied himself for some time now. As his thoughts wandered back to the encounter, his body reacted. "Calm down, old boy—we will get there." Julius smiled as he felt the urges surge through his body.

Julius pulled up in front of the Omni, and popped open the trunk. The concierge service here was always excellent. "Mr. Dent." Julius recognized the bellhop immediately. "We were all pulling for you—we knew it wasn't you…no way!"

Julius smiled as he handed him his keys and a twenty. "Thanks—it's good to know that some people believed in me."

Julius walked into the hotel lobby, and on cue the concierge walked right over to him and handed him his room keys. "We are so happy to see you again. If there is anything that you need—just ask, you know that I will get it for you."

Julius nodded in approval, handed him a twenty, and walked toward the elevators. Julius noticed quite a few smiles and acknowledgements as he disappeared through the elevator doors. "I'll be glad when everything gets back to normal…whatever normal is." Julius got off the elevator and entered the Presidential Suite. His bags were already sitting neatly in front of the armoire. There was a bottle of champagne positioned in a clear bucket of crushed ice and a fresh bowl of fruit sitting on the table in front of the recliner. A red card with gold lettering was propped against the champagne bottle that read, FROM YOUR FRIENDS AT THE OMNI—ENJOY YOUR STAY.

Julius walked over, looked out the window, and took in the beauty of the night. "Guess I better order some room service before it gets too late." Julius walked over to the phone, but before he could reach down to pick it up, the phone rang.

"Mr. Dent, would you like me to order your favorite meal?"

Julius smiled as he recognized the concierge's voice. "Yes, thank you very much." Julius had always been treated well by the staff, but it was blatantly obvious that they were going out of their way to cater to him. Normally, he didn't like a lot of attention, but this time he was very willing to accept some extra tender, loving care. Julius took off his clothes and took a long, hot shower. As he was drying off, he remembered that he had told Pam that he would give her a call. "I'll just wait until after I finish eating—then I will call her." Julius put on his loungewear, grabbed a hand-full of grapes, and sat down in the recliner. Julius wasn't a big drinker, but looking at the water beading on that bottle of champagne put him one of those "why not" moods.

By the time room service delivered his meal, he had eaten all of the grapes and put a big dent in that bottle of champagne. "Damn—I should know better." Julius could feel the effect of the champagne as he stared at the food that was in front of him. He really didn't feel that hungry now, but he knew that he couldn't walk away from a porter-house steak, baked potato, and green beans; he didn't. After eating every single piece of food on the plate, Julius plopped back into the recliner. "That was just wrong!" Julius laughed at himself and patted his over-stuffed stomach. "I really need to get that guy to work in one of my restaurants."

Julius looked over at the clock; it was 9:00 p.m. "I better call Pam before it gets too late…and before I doze off." Julius reached over, grabbed his cell phone, and called Pam.

"Hey you, did I catch you at a bad time?"

"Hello, Julius. No, I just got out of the shower and was sitting here relaxing." Pam certainly wasn't going to tell him that she had been waiting for his call all evening and that she had been thinking about him ever since she had talked to him earlier. "How was your flight?"

Julius paused for a moment. "I ran into a news reporter that I had promised to give an interview."

"I'm sorry, that must have been uncomfortable for you."

"No, actually, she turned out to be very understanding. In fact she refused the interview and said that I had been through enough."

Pam raised her eyebrow. She wanted to ask more about this person, but did not want Julius to detect that she may be feeling a little jealous. "Well, that was really nice of her."

Julius could hear the change in Pam's voice and decided that he better put her at ease. "I wanted to thank her after we landed at the airport, but after seeing how big Don Jetton was in person, I decided to skip the pleasantries."

"Don Jetton?" Pam asked.

"You know, the defensive end for the Chicago Bears."

"Oh, OK." Pam had no idea who this person was and frankly, didn't care. She was just happy to hear that this reporter was with a professional athlete and not after Julius.

Julius felt a little bit guilty that he hadn't really told the whole truth, but he felt that since he and Pam really weren't on that level yet, he really shouldn't divulge that to her. Yet, he still felt that he had not been honest, and he really didn't like that at all.

"Did you have a good day?" Julius wanted to get to the business at hand, and that was to get to know this lady.

Pam, feeling more at ease now, opened up and started back where they left off during the earlier conversation. Julius and Pam talked and talked. It was quite obvious to the both of them that they were so very comfortable with each other and that they had grown to like each other enough to possibly explore something more.

Julius glanced over at the clock; 12:30 a.m. "Hey, it's getting late, and I have a meeting at 10:00 a.m., so I better go."

Pam was surprised that they had talked for so long. She felt as if they had only been talking for a little while. "Oh, I'm sorry, Julius. I didn't mean to keep you up so late."

"No, I enjoy talking with you, and if I didn't have to get up in the morning, I would still be talking to you."

Pam smiled to herself; his words sounded like poetry to her ears. "OK, Mr. Dent. You get some rest."

"You too….hey, I'm flying out of here Sunday morning and heading for Baton Rouge. I'll be there for a few days, then on to Houston, San Antonio, and finally Memphis. Think about picking a city; I will get you a ticket and reserve you a room. I would love to have dinner with you away from the prying eyes of Atlanta."

"You know what, Julius, that really sounds like a good idea. I will check my schedule on Monday and get back with you."

Chapter 21

Pam looked out the window of the plane as a blur of runway lights zipped past. She was nervously excited about hooking up with Julius and wondered to herself whether they would be meeting as good friends, or whether they would push off into something more intimate. She thought about the nightly phone conversations that they'd had over the past couple of weeks and how wonderful it had been to have conversations with a man who wasn't intimidated by her position and power.

Pam took a deep breath as the plane finally pulled into the terminal. "OK, here we go." Pam grabbed her carry-on and walked anxiously across the ramp into the airport terminal. She immediately scanned the crowd of people, looking for Julius. She hadn't noticed that he had been standing and looking out the big glass window as the plane landed.

"Hey you," Julius whispered as he came up from behind her. Pam turned around and looked at Julius. She hesitated before she said anything. "What's wrong? Was the flight OK?"

Pam smiled at Julius. "They treated me like a queen." Julius smiled, as he embraced Pam and kissed her gently on the cheek.

"Welcome to San Antonio, Ms. Cooper." Julius grabbed Pam's bag and they started walking toward the baggage claim area. Pam was noticeably nervous as they stood waiting for her piece of luggage, and Julius could tell, so he gently took her hand in his, and they stood hand-in-hand until Pam's bag appeared on the carousel. Pam pointed out her bag, and Julius quickly grabbed it.

Julius turned toward Pam. "Don't worry. We are just here to have a good time and to enjoy some good food."

Pam inhaled deeply, relieved that Julius was being sensitive to her uneasiness. "OK, let's go." Pam tried to relax a little. She had to get used to the fact that she wasn't in Atlanta and no one was watching.

As they approached the front doors of the airport terminal, Julius turned to Pam. "It is really good to see you."

Pam smiled at Julius. "Thank you, and it is good seeing you too." To Pam's surprise, Julius had hired a limousine. The driver quickly walked over and took the bags from Julius. He welcomed Pam as he opened the door.

"And who are you trying to impress?"

Julius sat down close to Pam. "You deserve this, and I want this for you." Julius and Pam talked the entire time until they arrived at the Hyatt on the river walk.

The valet service opened the door to the limo. "Hello, Mr. Dent." The young man handed Julius a set of room keys, and Julius in turn handed them to Pam; she just shook her head. "Well, I guess you just have it like that."

Julius handed the young man twenty, as he almost ran back to get the bags from the trunk of the limo. "While you are here with me, I want you to do nothing but relax."

Pam looked at Julius with admiration. She could tell that he was not putting on a show; it seemed so natural—so him. Julius grabbed her by the hand as they walked through the lobby to the elevator.

Julius told her that he had reserved her suite right next to his because he wanted to make sure that he would be near if she needed him. Julius walked with Pam to her suite door, and with perfect timing the young man arrived with her bags just as she was opening the door. Julius thanked the young man and pulled Pam's bag inside. Pam looked around the room and nodded in satisfaction. "Pretty nice, Mr. Dent." Pam walked over to the window and looked down at the picturesque view of people walking along the lighted river walk path.

"I hope you like it."

Pam turned around to face Julius. "Yes, I like everything."

Julius looked at Pam standing there. She was the kind of sexy that attracted him. The kind of sexy that shows even when you are not trying. The kind of sexy that a real man searches for. "I know that you are tired from the flight. I made us late restaurant reservations, but I can cancel them if—"

Pam interrupted, "No—let's go, but before we do anything else..." Pam walked over, put her arms around Julius's neck and kissed him.

"I just wanted to get that one out of the way." As they walked out of the room, Pam could feel that tingling sensation; she knew that she would not be able to resist temptation—or fate.

Pam and Julius were silent the entire ride down the elevator. When the elevator doors opened, they both stared intensely at each other, but neither moved. Julius reached over and pushed the button. The doors closed and the elevator made its way back up.

"Give me fifteen minutes." Pam opened the door to her suite and slipped inside as Julius disappeared behind the door of his own suite. Pam walked over and opened her luggage. She stared down at the neatly arranged clothing that she had taken extra care to strap down tight. She had already imagined what she would wear if this opportunity presented itself; so she picked up the two-piece black silk set with the lace trim. She laid the outfit neatly on the bed, pulled out her toiletries and headed for the shower.

* * *

Julius looked at himself in the mirror as he dried off his body. He was somewhat disappointed as he noticed that he had lost some definition in his muscle tone. "Dang, I really need to get back to my old workout routine." Julius was just being hard on himself—his body would make most men his age very jealous. Besides, he had never been that very concerned about it anyway; he had always been annoyed when he would go to the gym and see guys so impressed with themselves that they totally ignored all those beautiful women that were all but laughing as those idiots adored themselves. Julius smiled as he rubbed himself down with some cocoa butter lotion. He slipped on some loungewear and sat down in the recliner. Julius was nervous but excited. He wasn't sure of why this was actually happening, but what he was sure of was that it had seemed almost inevitable almost from the first time he saw Pam in the courtroom.

Julius took a deep breath as the phone rang. "Hello." Julius strained to disguise any hint of nervousness. Pam invited Julius over. Julius reached into his bag, pulled out two condoms, and walked next door. Pam had already propped the door with the security latch so that Julius could come in, but being the consummate gentleman, he knocked and waited for Pam to tell him to enter.

"Come in, Julius." Julius came in and his mouth almost fell wide open as he saw Pam standing there in a stunning black lingerie set. The top was loose fitting, but couldn't hide the perfect roundness and obvious firmness of Pam's breasts. The bottoms were formfitting with lace that wrapped around Pam's thighs in perfect contrast to her silky smooth skin. This was not the same conservative woman that he had seen in the courtroom and certainly not the same woman that he remembered lying in the hospital bed. Julius had always thought that Pam was attractive, but he wasn't prepared for this.

"Something wrong?" Pam teasingly asked.

"I'm sorry, Pam; I don't mean to stare, but you are gorgeous!"

Pam smiled sheepishly. "You are too kind, Julius."

Julius walked over to Pam. "No, I really mean it—you have a perfect body."

Pam shook her head no as she pointed to the stab wound on her side. Julius took his finger and ran it along the length of the scar. "And this, to me, makes you all the more perfect." Julius took Pam into his arms and passionately kissed her. He felt his stomach twist and turn as he pulled Pam close to him. He was surprised at the warmth, softness, and gentleness of her kiss, the tenderness of her touch. Pam pulled back from Julius, grabbing her stomach.

"What's wrong?" Julius was concerned that maybe he had held her too tightly or was moving too fast.

"Nothing—it's just that, well—you are making me feel things that I have never felt before and…"

Julius walked over, picked Pam up in his arms, and carried her over to the bed. "Don't worry, Pam, I've got this." Julius took his time with Pam. Although it had been a long time since he had been with a woman, he knew that she needed tender love and care. For six hours Julius and Pam pleased each other gently. They allowed each other the opportunity to experience the pleasures of intimacy and the enjoyment of companionship, something they both so desperately needed.

"You OK?" Julius could feel the tears falling from Pam's eyes and sliding down his chest.

"I'm sorry, Julius."

Julius looked at Pam, "What is it?"

"Don't worry, they are happy tears."

Julius smiled and pulled Pam close to him. "This is much more than what I expected, Pam. I thought that this would eventually happen between you and me, but I never imagined that it would be like this." Pam looked into Julius's eyes and just like the first time, could see right through to his soul. He was so genuine and sincere. Pam snuggled close to Julius and enjoyed the warmth that their bodies created. She inhaled deeply, pleased by the scent that their bodies created together. They fell asleep in each other's arms—the first peaceful sleep for Julius since the day his wife died.

Chapter 22

The nurse ran almost frantically from Brenda's room. She was out of breath by the time she made it to the nurse's station. She screamed for the charge nurse to call Dr. Jamison. "What's wrong?"

The nurse could barely get anything out of her mouth. "You have got to see this."

The two nurses hurried back to Brenda's room. The charge nurse gasped in horror. "Oh shit!" She turned and ran back toward the nurse's station. As she approached she could see Dr. Jamison walking briskly toward her.

"What's the problem?" The charge nurse just shook her head from side to side and motioned for the doctor to follow her back to Brenda's room. As Dr. Jamison walked into Brenda's room, she slapped her hands over her mouth and gasped. "What have we done?"

House-cleaning had started to sanitize Brenda's room. When they removed the mattress from the bed they found several pills, messages, and notes on blood-stained tissue stuffed between the mattresses. On the headboard was blood-stained scribbling—words describing anger, pain, and despair. Dr. Jamison dropped to her knees as the magnitude of the situation slammed hard in her head. "Do we know where she is?" Both nurses shook their head no in unison. Dr. Jamison had signed Brenda's release papers the previous day; Brenda had packed and left within two hours of the papers being signed. She had told them that she had already made arrangements and would not need them to do anything for her. When the staff asked where she would go, she had responded that she would find a place here locally.

"Well, Valdosta is not that big; she will turn up sooner or later." Dr. Jamison walked out of the room, disappointed that Brenda had been clever enough to hide what was going on in her head all of these years. She knew that Brenda was sick and from what she had just seen, a danger to herself and maybe others.

The charge nurse walked next to Dr. Jamison and asked, "Do you want me to call the authorities?"

Dr. Jamison looked at both of the nurses. "And have this whole place investigated? You know we can't afford that." They all knew that reporting this would put their facility under intense scrutiny, and most of all they would all risk losing their licenses. "For now, let's just keep this one under wrap. If Brenda's problem is that bad, we will hear from her. She won't be able to function on her own for long. Besides, she has no one to depend on, especially now that her sister is dead." They all agreed not to speak about Brenda to anyone and went back to their normal daily routines.

* * *

Brenda clutched the big brown envelop tightly in her hand as she sat in the lobby of the Greyhound bus terminal. She looked down teary-eyed at Denise's handwriting on the envelope. She was almost reluctant to open it, but Denise had gone over this with her a million times.

"Sweetie you have to remember to keep this hidden from everyone. You won't need it unless something happens to me, but make sure that you are at the bus station before you open it—then take as much time as you need to make sure that you understand everything." Denise had pounded this into Brenda's brain, and she had done everything that her big sister had told her to do. Inside the big envelope was a long letter, four separate sets of keys, and ten one hundred dollar bills. Brenda started reading the letter.

> Hey little sis,
> I'm so very proud of you for getting out of that place. I knew that we could pull it off. Since you are reading this letter, that probably means that something has happened to me, and I'm so sorry that I can't be there with you. I just want you to know that you are ready to be out on your own. Remember everything that I taught you and remember to trust yourself more than you trust anyone else. You have to take care of everything, just like we discussed. It will be easy for you. I have left you the name and addresses of your bank. There will be three hundred thousand from mom and dad's insurance policy and whatever is left from what I managed to save. I'm sorry that I had to use some of the money, but I bought you a small condominium in Atlanta. It's not much, but it is fully furnished, paid for, and is yours. The utilities

are on and are paid automatically through your account. The address and keys are in the envelope. I also left you the keys and address to our house in Valdosta, just in case you decide to stay there. I know that you don't have a driver's license, but you do have a car as well. Just take your time, and teach yourself in the evening time in the local neighborhoods. When you feel comfortable, you can get your license. The small keys are to your safe deposit box at the bank; all of your important papers are there. The most important thing for you to remember is that you must trust yourself before anyone else. You can do this.
Love you always,
Dee Dee

    Brenda took the money from the bag and stuffed it in her pocket. She looked at the envelope with the address for her condo in Atlanta. She knew that she wouldn't be able to stay here in Valdosta for any time, especially since she knew that Dr. Jamison would surely figure out that she had been tricked into believing that she was well. Besides, she knew that the house here had nothing but bad memories, and she wanted no part of that. She also knew that she needed to be in Atlanta; yes, that was where she needed to be. Brenda folded the envelope, put it in her pocket and placed the big envelope back in her bag. She walked calmly to the ticket counter and purchased a one-way ticket to Atlanta. The ticket agent told her that the bus would be leaving in one hour and that they would call for boarding fifteen minutes prior to departure.

    As Brenda walked back to her seat, a flood of thoughts rushed through her mind. She remembered all the things that her sister had talked to her about over the years, about how she should carry herself as a young lady. She remembered how her sister had taught her to style her hair, wear makeup, and keep herself safe from men. She thought of the countless hours her sister had gone over schoolbooks with her, helping her perfect her reading, writing, and math skills. She had taught her how to write checks, balance a checkbook, and use an ATM card. She had taught her to use her good looks to her advantage. She had pounded in her head to never allow anyone or anything get to her; she wanted her to be stronger and less vulnerable to people that intended to do her harm. Brenda sat down and started to cry. She had been waiting on the day that she would be able to leave that place for years and was deeply saddened that she could not be with the one person who had stood by her side—the only person that she had to love and loved her unconditionally. Then, thoughts of vengeance filled her mind. She bit down hard on the inside of her lip until she tasted her blood. She knew that she would have to adjust quickly to being on her own because she had many things to do, many people to meet, and…

"BUS TWO TWELVE TO ATLANTA IS NOW BOARDING." Brenda's thoughts were interrupted by the announcement on the intercom system. Brenda stood up, walked quickly outside, and boarded the bus. She was one of the first to board, so she picked a window seat right in the front of the bus behind the driver, so that she could sit quietly and carefully observe each person as they passed by.

She hadn't been around a lot of people so she was trying her best to study how people acted and reacted. At the bus station she had noticed the many different facial expressions, fake smiles, and flirtatious demeanors of some of the young men. She noticed the different ways that the girls were dressing—some were conservative, others very provocative. She knew immediately that she wanted to be somewhere in between. Her sister had always said that if you show just a hint, it would make the ladies jealous and the men wild. Her mind tired from the barrage of thoughts; Brenda settled back in her seat and prepared herself for the ride and anticipation of her new life in Atlanta.

She closed her eyes for a moment, and then opened them. "I guess this is not a dream." Brenda stared out the window, looking all the things that she had missed over the years. She was enjoying her new sense of freedom. She tried not to think too much about what she had to do in Atlanta; first she wanted to enjoy just being free.

Chapter 23

Brenda stood and stared at the address. She had never heard of Buckhead. "What kind of name is that?" She smiled widely as she walked toward the door to her condo. "Number fifty-six twenty-one, I guess this is it." Brenda stuck the key in the door and slowly turned it. She held her breath, closed her eyes, and slowly opened the door. As she opened her eyes, she gasped. Denise had decorated her place just the way Brenda had described when they would sit for hours imagining how her home would be when she got out. Denise never told her that she was going to do this. The rooms were painted in her favorite color, peach. Denise had obviously put a lot of time and effort into Brenda's place, because no detail had been missed. This was the place that Brenda had dreamed about. For a moment Brenda forgot about everything.

Brenda walked from room to room, enjoying the details that her sister had transformed from her imagination to this reality. Brenda looked in the closet of her master bedroom; it was completely filled with very nice clothes and wall-to-wall shoes. Brenda laughed aloud as she rummaged through every outfit and tried on shoe after shoe. Her dresser was filled with lingerie and everything that she would ever need to make herself feel as beautiful as a queen. The bathroom was filled with toiletries, plush towels, and big white throw rugs.

Brenda walked back in her bedroom and lay across her bed. She stared at the ceiling. "Thanks, Dee Dee. I love it—simply love it!" Brenda was in an unfamiliar city, an unfamiliar house, and didn't know anyone; yet, she felt like she belonged here. "I know that you are here with me, big sis. Don't worry, I'm going to really make you proud of me...very proud." Brenda closed her eyes, and for the first time in what seemed like forever, she drifted into a deep sleep, a sleep without the haunting nightmares. It was as if she had left everything back in Valdosta.

Brenda slept for seven uninterrupted hours. When she awakened, she lay there and smiled that she didn't have to pretend anymore; she could be who she wanted to be and express herself how she chose. Brenda sat up in bed. "Well, I probably should go ahead and get started." Brenda pulled off her clothes and walked to the bathroom. She stopped and looked at herself in the mirror. She remembered how her sister would always tell her how beautiful she was and how one day men would die for her.

"Yes, they will." Brenda realized exactly what her sister meant as she stared down her reflection. She had never really looked at herself like this before. She had inherited her mother's light brown eyes and facial features, but her body—well, it was in perfect proportion, just like her father, who had been very athletic all of his life. Brenda marveled at how perfectly round her breasts were and how smooth her skin was. She turned around and looked at her flawless butt. "Yes, they certainly will die for a piece of this." Brenda laughed as she stepped into the shower. She knew that she had a lot of catching up to do. Although Denise had taught her much, she knew that she had much more to learn. She needed to be able to fit in, be able to be noticed, but not stand out as odd. She needed to practice being normal, something that would take a lot for her because she was far from normal.

After getting cleaned up, Brenda put on a gown and walked around familiarizing herself with her new home. She saw that her pantry was full of canned goods, but the refrigerator was empty. She picked up the phone and was happy to hear a dial tone. She looked in the phonebook to call a taxi, but thought twice. "Maybe I should just walk the neighborhood to see if there is a city bus that runs this way." Brenda glanced at herself in the mirror and shook her head in approval at how well her new clothes fit. She stuffed some money in her pocket, grabbed her door key, and headed out the door. She knew that she had a car somewhere, but she knew that she was not ready for that.

Brenda walked one block up the street and turned left. "I will just walk this block and see what's up." As she turned down the second street, she smiled as she saw a bench and sign that read "CITY TRANSIT." She also could see that there was a strip mall a little further down the road, and she could see a Publix Supermarket sign. "Bingo!" Brenda smiled as she realized that her sister had made sure that she was within walking distance of a shopping center. Brenda spent the next four hours walking and looking in stores. She was having a wonderful time just looking at people. She had been approached by no less than ten men, trying to strike up conversation. She never spoke to them, though, just smiled and kept doing what she was doing. She carefully studied mannerisms and how people interacted with each other. Finally, tired and hungry, Brenda shopped for groceries and had customer service call for her taxi. By the time she made it back home and put up her groceries, she was worn out. She put a frozen pizza in the oven and rushed to take another shower.

"I can't believe that I am here doing this by myself." Brenda, almost teary-eyed, wondered how it would be if she had her sister here with her. She thought of all the things that they could have done together, now that she was old enough to hang out with her. Brenda shook off her feelings; she knew that she needed to concentrate more on what she had now, than what could have been. She finished her shower, put on a comfortable nightgown and hurried to take her pizza out of the oven. Brenda sat down at the table and started to eat. She realized that she had not turned on a television to see if they worked. She grabbed the remote. "All righty then!" Brenda was ecstatic to see that the television did work and that there was cable. She snacked and looked at television until she dozed off on the sofa; however, this time sleep didn't come without residuals.

Brenda's body twisted and turned as flashes of painful memories and thoughts of death crept through every crevice in the deepest folds of her mind. She dreamt of men chasing, catching, and right as they ripped her panties from her body, she awakened. Brenda was confused as she opened her eyes. Her hand was in her panties and her fingers were buried deep inside her unblemished folds. She was both surprised and scared of what she was feeling but knew that it was one of the things that her sister had described. Unknowingly, Brenda had unleashed her beast. She had found desire—untamed and unmanageable desire.

Feeling dirty and ashamed, Brenda got up and hurried to take a shower. As the hot water beat down on her, she felt the urge to touch herself again—and she did—again, and again, until her body was completely overwhelmed by rush after rush of pure pleasure. Brenda forced herself out of the now cold shower. She dried herself off trying desperately not to disturb her overly swollen newfound friend. She dragged herself to the bed, crawled under the sheet, and fell fast asleep. It wasn't long before she was dreaming the same dream again, but this time, her mind had adjusted. She told the men that they didn't have to take it and that it would be better if she gave it to them. One by one, Brenda led each man into a dark room. Each time she returned, she would track footprints of blood. When she came back, the last man was facing toward a window. When she tapped him on the shoulder and he turned around, she plunged a knife deep into his neck—it was her father. Brenda sat straight up in bed, but she was not frightened; she giggled to herself. "Now I know what I'm supposed to do." Brenda lay down and drifted off into a deep, peaceful sleep.

Brenda rested her busy mind for the rest of the night. She awakened the next morning feeling refreshed and ready to start her day. She sat up in bed and looked around the room. She laughed aloud. "This is a whole lot better than that shithole that I stayed in for half my damn life." She got up and walked over to the stack of papers that her sister had left her. She picked up the papers, found a notebook and pen, and walked directly to the kitchen. She sat down at the kitchen table and studied the letter that Denise had carefully written. She looked at each item and wrote down exactly what she needed to do to.

"OK, looks like I should go to the bank to inspect the items in the safe deposit box first; then, I should go find the garage where Denise has stored my car; then I should make my way to find where my sister used to live; and last, and finally, I need to look for a way to get close to Julius Dent." Brenda smiled as she realized what she was about to do. She knew that this was the start of an adventure—a script that she would create and control.

Chapter 24

Pam opened her eyes and looked over at the man sleeping peacefully beside her. She smiled as she heard the soft rumbling of snoring. "Not perfect after all." She giggled to herself, and then sighed deeply. For one of the few times in her life, she felt content. She felt, well, happy. Pam settled deep into the pillow and allowed herself to enjoy her moment. She wondered how long this moment would last, how long it would be before reality came rushing in. She thought about all that had happened over the last couple of years, the events that had led to her lying in bed beside the very man that she had vowed to put away for life. She looked over at Julius. "I was so very wrong." Pam reached over and ran her fingers down the side of Julius's face.

He slowly opened his eyes. "Hey you," Julius whispered.

Without saying a word, Pam pulled back the covers and straddled Julius. She leaned over and kissed his chest gently, Julius's body responded immediately. Pam slowly and methodically took them away, away to a place they both longed for, a place called ecstasy. Pam knew that this was much more than just sex; it was better, was deeper, deeper than anything she had ever felt before. Pam's body tensed as she reached her destination. Julius pulled her down on him and held her tightly as her body jerked from her moment of peak satisfaction. Pam whispered, "Your turn."

Julius shook his head. "No, this is exactly what I want, for you to be happy and satisfied." He lay there and allowed Pam to have uninterrupted sensations of bliss.

Pam looked at the clock on the bedside table. "You know we have to get ready to go." Julius nodded a reluctant yes. Pam kissed Julius teasingly on his lips and gently rolled off him. She walked over to the chair where she had left her clothes and quickly slipped them on. "I will be ready in about thirty minutes." Pam walked seductively out of the room as Julius smiled holding his chest, mocking the hurt she was causing by leaving. Julius reached over, picked up the phone, and called the front desk. He wanted to make sure that they had reserved the limo to go back to the airport. After he confirmed that all was in order, he got up, took his shower, and started packing his things.

Julius's mind was traveling down a road that he thought would be under construction for much longer, but the road seemed to be perfectly paved. He knew that he would occasionally run into a pothole, but as far as his mind could see, there should be nothing to slow down this journey. Julius had just closed his last bag when Pam knocked on the door. She smiled when Julius opened the door and she saw that he was just as punctual as she. Julius looked down at his watch, and again on cue, a young man appeared, walking toward them to carry their luggage.

"Well, Mr. Dent, what now?"

Julius knew that they would have to plan their relationship carefully. Neither of them wanted to be back in the limelight anytime soon. "We will just take our time and be careful who we allow to know about us. In time, things will settle down enough that it won't matter."

Pam nodded her head in agreement. "We will make it work." Julius gave Pam a reassuring smile as the elevator doors closed and they readied themselves for a clandestine relationship.

As the limousine pulled into the airport, Julius leaned over and kissed Pam. "Don't worry, we will be fine." Pam looked into Julius's eyes. She wanted to believe that their newfound relationship would grow into something more than just weekend getaways or secret meetings. She knew that only time would allow them to have an open relationship. It simply had not been enough time between all that had happened and them getting together. They both knew that the media would eat them alive.

"For now, this is best for both of us." They both nodded their heads in agreement as they checked their luggage. Julius had booked separate flights for them. Pam's flight was scheduled to depart in twenty minutes, so they both walked quickly through the terminal. By the time they arrived at the gate, first class passengers were boarding. Julius and Pam hugged each other tightly and said their goodbyes. Pam pulled away and walked briskly through the walkway to the plane. She wanted to, but did not dare turn around. Her eyes were full of tears, and she did not want to look back at her new lover.

Pam found her seat quickly, sat down, and buried her face in her hands. A flight attendant approached and asked if everything was all right. Pam looked up at her, tears racing down her cheeks. "Believe it or not, everything is wonderful." The flight attendant cocked her head to the side and smiled as she handed Pam a handful of tissues. "I'll check on you later." The flight attendant went on with her duties.

* * *

Julius watched as the plane backed away from the terminal. He couldn't help but get a little emotional. Although he knew that they would see each other soon, he wondered if they would really be able to pull this relationship off. They would have to work diligently to make this work and to keep out of the public eye. Julius took a long, deep breath as ticket agents made the first boarding call for this flight. Just as they called for first class boarding, Julius looked over to his right; there standing and staring was Cynthia LaMay. Julius's heart started racing. He wondered whether she had seen him with Pam. Julius almost froze as she walked toward him.

"What a coincidence." Cynthia seemed a bit condescending.

Julius decided to play it cool. "Hey, I've been thinking about you." Cynthia was caught off guard. "I wanted to apologize to you about—"

Cynthia stopped Julius in mid-sentence. "Don't—nothing happened that I didn't want to happen…and don't worry, I don't kiss and tell. Now, you go ahead and board, maybe I will see you sometime in Atlanta."

Julius smiled at Cynthia. He wasn't sure whether she had seen him with Pam, but he was somewhat sure that she was no threat to him. "I'm really going to do something special for her," Julius thought to himself as he boarded the plane. Julius knew that Pam was special because he didn't think twice about how formfitting the jeans were on Cynthia or how sexy she looked as she walked toward him. No, Julius was still thinking about how comfortable he had felt with Pam and how he couldn't wait until they were together again.

Julius settled back into his seat as the rest of the passengers passed by. This had been a successful business trip for him. He had strengthened his business alliances and solidified commitments that would assure that Dent Enterprises could continue to grow and prosper. Julius was almost oblivious as the plane backed away from the gate and the flight attendants started their pre-flight speeches and preparation.

"I'm getting back into my rhythm now—my groove." Julius smiled as the plane's powerful momentum pushed him deeper into the soft leather seat and lifted gently into the air. He closed his eyes and relished the almost complete feeling of satisfaction. Julius had not experienced this feeling for such a long time. He had often wondered, with all of the turmoil, whether he ever would. He knew that getting this business out of the way would give him some relief, but he never would have guessed that Pam could create such a sense of peace in him.

Julius, his mind at ease, fell asleep. This for him was a first. In all of his travels, he had never fallen asleep on a plane; he had always been vigilant since 911. He never wanted to be caught off guard. He knew that he would rather die fighting than sitting back and allowing someone to dictate how he would die.

* * *

Julius's eyes popped wide open. He could feel himself being pressed deep into his seat again. He heard screams and felt the plane jerking wildly; he realized that they were in a nosedive. He looked around as air masks dangled like Christmas ornaments all around him. Julius reached down and pulled his seatbelt tightly. He didn't panic as he looked out of the window of the plane, seeing the blurry image of greenery growing ever so clearer as the plane raced toward its destiny. Julius did not speak a word; he simply closed his eyes as the plane plunged. Just as the plane reached the top of the tree line, Julius opened his eyes.

"Damn—what was that all about?" Julius awakened. He was startled, but happy that he had just been dreaming. Julius put his hand on his chest and felt his heart pounding. He had only had disturbing dreams like the ones in the weeks prior to Tiara's murder. It had taken him a long time to remember that he had dreamed those dreams and had taken him twice as long to forget. Julius tried, but couldn't shake the feeling that something was going to happen…something bad was going to happen. "Man—what is going on with me?" Julius tried to relax as the plane prepared for landing. "I hope Pam is OK. I will call her as soon as I get off the plane."

Julius was very anxious as he walked through the tunnel into the terminal. He reached for his cell phone and quickly found the speed dial for Pam.

"Hello," Pam's reassuring voice answered the phone.

"Hey you. I just wanted to call to make sure that you made it home safely."

"I'm quite fine, Mr. Dent. I'm still riding on the high from our little excursion—I really don't want to come down."

Julius smiled as Pam's voice quickly calmed him and the uneasy feeling subsided. "Yeah, I've been thinking about it too. I'm very happy that we finally made this connection. Pam, can I tell you something?"

Pam paused as she could detect the seriousness in Julius's voice. "Sure Julius, what is it?"

"Well, I really see something special in you. I know that this was the very first time that we have been together, but I just want you to know that I'm not seeing anyone else. I really haven't since Tiara…I guess what I'm trying to say is that I really want us to have an exclusive relationship." Julius paused. "Do you think that I'm rushing things?"

Pam closed her eyes and took a second to let Julius's words penetrate her soul. "Julius, I haven't been in a serious relationship for years. We have been through so much in such a short time. We connected. I don't know why we did, but that doesn't change the fact that we seem to fit. I would love to have an exclusive relationship with you, even though I know that it will be difficult since we will have to keep it out of the limelight for a while."

"Good, then I will call you later, after I get home and get settled." Julius had already made it to the luggage carousel and waited patiently as the red light started to flash and the big contraption started turning. He smiled as he quickly spotted his bag rolling toward him. He grabbed his bag and made his way to the parking garage.

Julius felt a whole lot better after talking to Pam. He thought to himself that the dream must have just been him wanting to make sure that Pam was safe, but in any case, he felt better now. Julius finally reached his car. He was ready to get home and relax. He wanted to take a long, hot shower, get something to eat, and then call Pam. He started his car, and like he had done so many times before, paused and listened to the smooth, powerful growl coming from the engine. The radio was set to his favorite "old school" station.

"Perfect." Julius sat and listened to the smooth, mellow beat. He shook his head. "They really don't make them like that anymore." Julius backed his car out and slowly drove away. He had always dreaded the trip from the airport—it had always seemed so mundane, but this time it didn't seem so very bad. He had his music playing, his business was in order, and he had a new relationship. "Things are finally back on track." Julius couldn't help but smile, realizing that he was absent of the empty feeling that had lingered with him since that dreadful night a few years ago. For such a long time his heart had been empty and hollow; now, he felt warm and invigorated. He had a sense of purposeful adventure, and Pam was the object of his affection.

Julius pressed the button on his garage door and pulled inside. He quickly gathered his things and went inside. Julius had developed a routine since he had been in his home alone. He would always walk through his entire house after he had been gone for a few days. Even though he had a very good security system, he would double check just to be safe. It wasn't paranoia, just being extra careful. He never wanted to be caught off guard again.

Sure that everything was in place, Julius took his bags to the bedroom to unpack. His mind drifted a bit as he remembered that Tiara would always unpack his bags for him after he returned from a trip. "I really miss that woman." Julius was somewhat surprised when he didn't get emotional thinking about Tiara. He was even more surprised that the very next thought in his mind was of Pam. He smiled, walked over to his bedside table, and grabbed his cell phone to call Pam. Just as he was about to call, the phone rang. "Hello." Julius smiled when he recognized Pam's voice on the other end.

"I know that you just got in, but I was thinking about you and wanted to know if I could see you before we have to go back to work tomorrow."

Julius didn't have to think about his answer, the growing bulge in his pants did that for him. "I was just thinking about you…my place or yours?"

"Why don't I come see you, Mr. Dent?"

"OK, I'll give you directions and open the garage for you when you get here."

Pam laughed. "I know where you live, Julius. Are you forgetting who you are talking to?"

Julius laughed. "I guess you would—yep, I guess you would."

It didn't take Pam long to get there. After she had spoken to Julius earlier in the day, she had already decided that she wanted to see him tonight and knew that he would say yes. As she pulled into his driveway, the garage doors slowly raised. Julius had been waiting and looking out for her arrival, so that she wouldn't have to wait to be able to pull inside. They both knew that at this point, no one should have any idea or reason to suspect they were a couple, so they were a little carefree, but still not blatantly open. Pam pulled her car carefully in and stared in her rearview mirror as the garage doors lowered. When she looked back forward, Julius was standing in the garage doorway with black silk bottoms and no shirt. The sight of Julius standing there took her breath away. She immediately felt moisture and a slight pulsing sensation. "Damn!"

At first Pam thought that maybe she should try not to appear too anxious; however, her body was screaming something else and her mind, this time, would not override what her body was telling her. Pam got out of the car and walked quickly over to Julius. Without hesitation, she kissed him wildly and pushed him backward into the house. She had never been inside Julius's house before and she was not looking for a tour. She pushed him up against the wall and continued kissing him until Julius's senses were in a frenzy. She jumped into is waiting arms and wrapped her legs around his waist as he held her tightly and walked toward his bedroom. Julius instinctively knew that this was not a time for passion, this was a time to let go and enjoy the excitement that Pam had created. He lay down on the bed and rolled so that she was on top of him. Pam stopped kissing Julius just long enough to pull her clothes off, and then she was at him again.

After two hours of blissful excitement, Pam drowned in her pool of ecstasy. She laid there next to Julius trying to catch her breath. "You OK?" Julius smoothed the hair back from her face.

"I guess I kind of got carried away—didn't see that one coming." Pam smiled as she realized that she had never, in her lifetime, been so into a man sexually. "I don't know what it is about you, Mr. Dent. You make me feel wild inside, and I've never been to that place before."

Julius looked over at Pam, and then turned on his side toward her. He ran his fingers lightly down her neck, across her breast. Pam's body trembled as Julius rolled over on top of her.

"What kind of man are you? You can't possibly still..." Pam gasped as Julius changed the pace of their encounter into a slow, methodical experience of lovemaking.

"You are going to have to call in for work...we are going to be a while." Pam smiled as Julius took her away on a magic carpet ride, one that lasted until well after the sun came up, one that would leave an indelible impression for life.

Pam laid there, her body and mind exhausted, yet relaxed and content. She thought about going through her routine for stress relief, but there was no stress to be found. She turned and looked at Julius who was still resting after his marathon of lovemaking and obvious statement of sexual superiority. Pam thought to herself of how quiet and gently powerful Julius had been in their lovemaking. She somehow knew that he had always been this way with women. As she looked at him, she noticed how peaceful he looked. She thought, "How could I have been so wrong to judge this man...he would never have hurt his wife."

Pam slowly got out of bed, trying her best not to disturb Julius. She walked into the master bathroom and closed the big white French doors behind her. "Nice." Pam hadn't really seen Julius's house yet and hadn't noticed how exquisitely decorated it was. Everything was neatly arranged and perfectly coordinated. Pam quickly found the towels and stepped down into the shower. The shower was open with black ceramic tile on the floor and walls. There were two separate showerheads with built-in massage controls. Pam turned the water on and adjusted the temperature until it was just the way she liked it. She stood under the water and cooed as the pulsation beat down on her shoulders and back. She closed her eyes and enjoyed the hot water massage. When she opened her eyes, Julius was standing just outside the shower. He had a bottle of therapeutic bath gel in his hand.

"Mind if I join you?" Pam just smiled and motioned for him to come in.

Julius stood behind Pam and gently spread the bath gel on her shoulders. He massaged her shoulders and back. The aroma of the gel, combined with Julius's masterful hands, was almost too much.

Julius gave the bottle to Pam so that she could finish taking her shower and turned on the second showerhead so that he could do the same. Pam found it strange but pleasing that she and Julius were taking a shower together and not speaking with words, but with subtle eye contact and meaningful facial expressions. Julius intentionally finished his shower before Pam. He got out of the shower, hurriedly dried off and disappeared into the closet. As Pam finished her shower and dried off, Julius reappeared wearing a black terrycloth robe with the initials "JD" embroidered on the collar. Draped over his arm was a burgundy terrycloth robe with the same embroidered initials. He walked over and wrapped Pam in the robe. She was pleasantly surprised to see that Julius had warmed the robe. "How nice."

Pam smiled widely at Julius as he walked her out of the bathroom, down the hallway, and into the breakfast area. For the first time, Pam was getting a good look of how Julius was living, and it was impressive. She didn't want to appear in awe so she just took in the view and waited to see what Julius had planned. Julius walked Pam over to a big window with two big chaises positioned in front of a window. "Why don't you relax—I brought your cell so that you can call in…or at least tell them you will be late." Julius smiled as he handed Pam her cell phone and walked toward the kitchen.

Pam, anxious to see what Julius was going to do next, quickly called her secretary. "Mae, what do I have on my schedule for today?"

Mae hesitated for a second as she looked down Pam's docket and meeting agenda schedule. "Looks like you have a couple of in-house meetings with the assistants but nothing pressing is on the docket that John can't handle."

"Good, I won't be coming in today."

"Are you all right? You don't quite sound like yourself this morning."

Pam knew that this would be coming. Mae would never miss an opportunity to pry into Pam's business. "I'm fine, Mae; I just had a busy weekend and didn't get enough rest, so I'm taking the day to relax. I will be back in tomorrow. If there is anything that comes up that John can't handle, just call me." Pam quickly ended the call before Mae could continue to dig. Pam's senses were aroused as she heard a grinding noise coming from the kitchen area. She almost immediately smelled the undeniable scent of coffee beans and after about two or three minutes, the entire room was filled with an intoxicating aroma.

    A few minutes later, Julius walked up carrying a beautiful dark-stained wood tray that was filled with two plates of eggs, bacon, biscuits, a carafe of coffee, two cups, cream, and a sugar bowl. He placed the tray in between them. "A little something for the soul." Julius smiled at Pam as her eyes gleamed. Pam was almost disappointed as Julius reached for a remote. She didn't want to ruin this moment with television, but to her surprise, the remote was to the big curtains that covered the window that they were sitting in front of. The curtains pulled back slowly and revealed a picturesque view of Julius's backyard, which was neatly trimmed and lined with colorful flowers, and with a path lined by two rows of perfectly pruned bushes.

    "Well, I didn't expect this from you, Mr. Dent." Pam got up, walked over, and stood up at the window. She stared out and almost gasped at the deep green color of the grass and almost perfect contrast of the flowers.

    "Come on back here before your food gets cold." With that, Pam walked back over to the chaise and sat down facing Julius. She started with the coffee. Julius was careful to watch how much sugar and cream she used so that he would know exactly how she liked it from now on. Pam sipped from the cup, closed her eyes and shook her head slowly. "There is absolutely nothing like freshly ground coffee." Pam then took a forkful of eggs and bit a piece of bacon. She didn't have to say word; her facial expression said it all. Julius knew that he could cook and believed that anyone in the restaurant business that couldn't cook shouldn't be in the business. Convinced that Pam was enjoying her meal, Julius joined in.

    "That was very good, sir." Pam smiled at Julius with admiration. "I have never had a man cook for me, so not only is this a first, but to have someone put it down like that; well, this ranks pretty dang high on my list."

    Julius smiled at Pam as he sipped on his coffee.

    "You really don't talk that much, do you?" Pam asked as Julius sat back on his chaise.

    "I've never really been a big talker. Don't get me wrong, when I have to get it done, I am the talker, but when I'm in my own element, I think much more than I talk. This is where I can be me and not have to worry about the pressures that come along with who I am or what I do."

Pam sat back and relaxed on her chaise. "That sounds a lot like how I feel too. It's hard having to be a certain way around people at work. You really can't afford to let your guard down, so you tend to be a lot more reserved when you are out of that environment."

"Exactly!" Julius felt good that Pam understood where he was coming from. This was one of the things that he had liked about Pam—she seemed to get it, to understand the difference between the persona and the man, and that was so very important for Julius. Julius looked over at Pam and could see that her eyes were closed. He pressed the remote and the curtains slowly closed. They didn't need to say a word; they both lay on the chaises and fell asleep.

Chapter 25

Brenda smiled widely as the DMV clerk took her picture. "I did it!" Brenda was happy that she now had a driver's license. She had taken lessons and had passed both the written and driving tests on the first attempt. Brenda took her new driver's license and walked quickly out to her car. She had been lucky that she had charmed her way out of proving that she had not driven herself there without a license. "Hell, all it took was a little high skirt action." She laughed loudly as she carefully drove off and headed toward her place in Buckhead. Riding the city transit had helped her immensely with her sense of direction. She had become familiar with all of Buckhead and most of Atlanta. She knew that she could find her way back to either condo from most anywhere in the city and now that she was finally able to drive legally, she knew that she would be able to go everywhere without time limitations.

Brenda had become an expert at being inconspicuous. She could produce an exotic look when she wanted, but blend in when she needed. Her confidence in dealing with people had increased tenfold, and she certainly felt no intimidation with big city life. Brenda sensed that everything was falling into place for her. Denise had left implicit guidance, and all of her business was in order. She had two condos, both paid for and fully furnished. She had a car, a complete wardrobe, and plenty of money in the bank. She had successfully transitioned to life here while remaining almost transparent in the community.

For the past three months she had spent countless hours in the library reading old news clippings and trying to find out as much as she could about Mr. Dent and Ms. Cooper. Now it was time to get closer to them, but first she wanted to taste death once again. She wanted to know whether it would haunt her as it had for so many years with her father. Although she rarely had dreams about her father anymore, she was still having vivid, violent dreams of sexual encounters leading to death—but now the dreams didn't keep her awake. They seemed to ease her mind and comfort her. All she knew was that it seemed as if her dreams came somewhat as a teacher and she, the student.

As Brenda pulled up in front of the condo, she thought to herself,

"I better tie up some loose ends in Valdosta before I get down to business here." Brenda realized that Dr. Jamison was probably fully aware that she had duped them into believing that she was all right, and may become suspicious hearing news of killings in Atlanta. She knew that the staff in that facility would be the only ones who could possibly get her caught since there was no one in the entire Atlanta region that knew she was Denise's little sister. She really wasn't concerned about the nurses and aides; her only concern was Dr. Jamison. She knew that she would likely be the one to contact the authorities.

"I need to find and destroy my file, and then destroy anyone who is a threat to exposing me." Brenda calmly got out of her car and walked briskly to her front door. As she turned the key she looked back, smiled, and did a little dance move in celebration of getting her license.

Brenda started peeling off her clothes as she walked through the front door. By the time she made it to her bedroom, she was down to panties and bra. She walked into her closet and thought, "I need to dress it up so they will at least have a difficult time recognizing me." Brenda pulled down a nice black pantsuit and a dark black hairpiece that she liked to wear when she would go to clubs in Atlanta. She went into her bathroom and put extra makeup on. She knew that they had only seen a bland little girl. They would never expect her to look like this, and by the time she was finished with her mini-makeover, she was right. Brenda had always been a cute girl while growing up; but she was a far cry from cute now. She had fully blossomed, was now a quite stunning young lady, and when she really tried, she could transform her look drastically. As she touched up her lipstick, she smiled at the reflection smiling back at her, reached up, and scribbled "LTD-R" on the mirror with her red lipstick. As she stared at the letters she realized that she had just created part of her modus operandi.

She smiled, grabbed her things, and headed back out to her car. "OK, it's eleven thirty, I have a full tank of gas, and I-75 south will take me straight to Valdosta. I should make it there by six o'clock, which will give me just enough time." Brenda had stayed in the facility for so long, she knew Dr. Jamison's schedule like the back of her hand. She was well aware that every Friday, Dr. Jamison would always stay at work until at least seven thirty to make sure that she made herself available before she took off for the rest of the weekend. "I hope that she hasn't changed her schedule. I would hate to have to track her ass down." Brenda drove off and headed for the interstate. "I am so glad that I'm leaving before rush hour; I would never make it there in time if it were any later."

Brenda's drive was uneventful. She had made it to Valdosta faster than she had anticipated. She had miscalculated the time and was sitting in the parking lot of the facility at five o'clock. She knew that most of the staff was getting off from work now so she figured that this would be a good time to see if anyone would recognize her. As people started walking out to their cars, she walked slowly toward the building. No one seemed to notice, but most all of the male employees stared her down, and of course she knew why. Brenda made it inside the building without anyone recognizing her. She knew this building inside out, the habits of the guards, all the places that they would be, and exactly when they would be there.

When she walked into the building, she took a quick right to the stairwell and walked up a flight of stairs to the second floor. She looked at her watch. "Five fifteen—she will be making her third floor rounds." Brenda quickly made her way to Dr. Jamison's office. Her office was near the stairwell, and the nurse's station was at the other end of the hall. She knew that at this time of the day, the nurses would most likely be congregating at the nurse's station, so there was little chance of her being seen. She walked into Dr. Jamison's office, being careful to make sure that she closed the door behind her. She walked immediately to the filing cabinet and searched for her file; it didn't take long for her to find it. A sheet of paper was stapled to the front of her file that read: "WARNING. CONTACT AUTHORITIES IF NOT LOCATED BY DECEMBER."

Brenda's mouth twitched as anger filled her. She bit down hard on the inside of her cheek until she sensed the familiar taste of her own blood. She sat the file down on top of the filing cabinet, sat down at the desk, and opened the top drawer. She saw that Dr. Jamison had an apple and paring knife in a plastic bag. She took the knife, walked over, and stood against the wall behind the door where she would not be seen when the door was opened. While she stood there, she grabbed the white coat that was hanging on the back of the door. She felt inside of the pocket and found a pair of latex gloves that she had seen Dr. Jamison take from her pocket thousands of times before. "This might get a little messy. I certainly don't want anyone to see blood all over me. That would not be good."

Brenda waited patiently until the door opened. She was hoping with all her might that this was not someone other than Dr. Jamison or that she wouldn't be alone. The door opened and Dr. Jamison walked in, alone. Without a word or a second thought, Brenda thrust the paring knife deep into the soft flesh of Dr. Jamison's neck and quickly put her hand over her mouth so that she could not scream, not realizing that she would not have been able to scream anyway. She had thrust the knife perfectly, piercing the carotid artery and severing her vocal cords instantly. Dr. Jamison's body slumped down to the floor causing Brenda to momentarily lose her balance as she tried desperately to keep the body from slamming hard to the floor. Brenda struggled but managed to drag her over and prop her up against the desk. The knife was still inside her neck, so there was not as much blood as Brenda had thought there would be. She grabbed her file from the top of the cabinet and knelt down in front of the doctor. She smiled when she saw that Dr. Jamison finally recognized her.

"You knew that I would be back, didn't you?" Brenda marveled at her terror-filled eyes, and waited and watched as the last signs of life drifted from her body. She grabbed Dr. Jamison's finger and pushed it onto the blood that had pooled down on the floor. She carefully printed the letters "LTD-R" on the floor right next to the body. Brenda knew that the authorities would think that Dr. Jamison was trying to give them the initials of who did this, but they would never know exactly what it meant. Brenda took off the white coat and put it back on the back of the door. She took off the gloves and stuffed them in her pocket. She slowly opened the door and looked both ways down the hall; the coast was clear. She had three minutes before the guard would make his way to lock the front doors. Brenda hurried down the stairs, paused, then walked calmly out the front doors and to her car. She laughed to herself as she slowly drove away.

"I better get out of town before I stop to gas up. Can't afford to make any mistakes." Brenda headed up I-75 back toward Atlanta…back toward her destiny.

Brenda was full of energy. She couldn't believe how exhilarated she felt. "That wasn't so bad. In fact, that was great!" Brenda saw the signs on the side of the road that she was approaching an exit with a gas station. "I better gas up now." Brenda scanned the front of the convenience store, checking for security cameras. Since she was relatively close to Valdosta, she needed to be careful, just in case the police would scan nearby gas stations' surveillance videos. Brenda fixed her hair so that it was covering most of her face. She was careful as she filled her car with gas to look down so that any surveillance cameras that she had not seen didn't get a direct view of her face. She finished pumping the gas and quickly drove away.

As she got back on the interstate, she realized that she still had the latex gloves in her pocket. "No souvenirs." She rolled down her window, checked her rearview mirror to make sure that no police were in sight, and tossed one glove out. She drove another fifteen minutes before she tossed the second.

She turned the volume down on her radio. "Can't hear myself think." Brenda relived the moment that she killed Dr. Jamison. The images in her mind kept replaying themselves over and over again. She smiled as she realized that she did not yet have the same haunting feelings that had stalked her with the death of her father. "Feels good, feels real good." Brenda spent the rest of her drive thinking, planning, dreaming of her next kill.

Chapter 26

Pam walked briskly toward her office, smiling and greeting everyone she came in contact with. Everyone noticed her upbeat and happy disposition. It's not that she was mean or rude; she had just always been about business and had never felt the need to exchange unnecessary fake pleasantries with the people at the office. She walked into her office and continued her grandioso smile and upbeat demeanor.

"Good morning, Mae." Pam grabbed a handful of notes and files from the box marked with her name and walked quickly to her office, and for the first time in years, did not close the door behind her. Simultaneously, everyone in the office looked at each other, puzzled over the bubbly, almost carefree stranger that had just walked through their office.

One of the clerks walked over to Mae. "What was that all about?"

Mae shrugged her shoulders. "I don't know. Let me do a little investigating." The ladies both smiled at each other as Mae walked over to pour Pam her morning cup of coffee.

Mae, almost reluctant to walk in Pam's rarely open door, knocked. "Pam, I have your coffee."

Pam looked up at her, smiling from ear to ear. "Come on in, Mae...and how are you this wonderful morning?"

Mae cocked her head sideways, somewhat like a puppy trying to figure out some weird sound. "Uhh—Pam, is everything all right?"

"Of course everything is all right. What are you talking about?"

Mae put the hot cup of coffee down in front of Pam. "Well, you are acting, sort of, you know..."

"Spit it out—what are you talking about?" Before Mae could say another word, Pam's cell phone started to vibrate. "Hey mister—I have someone in my office, can I call you later?" Mae, shocked but delighted, gave Pam one of those "you go, girl" looks and motioned for her to go ahead and talk. Mae walked quickly from the room, closing the door behind her.

The clerk quickly walked over to Mae. "So what did you find out?"

Mae leaned over and whispered, "Looks like someone is finally tapping that ass!" The ladies high-fived each other as they walked back to their desks.

"OK, Mr. Dent, how are you this morning?" Pam was delighted that Julius had called.

"I just wanted to hear your voice before I got too deep in my work this morning."

"Well, that is so sweet. Are you trying to win me over?"

"Well—yes, is it working?"

Pam paused for a moment then whispered, "Right now, my body is telling me that it's working a little too well!"

"Oh—my bad…guess I better get back to work before you make me want to leave. I will call you tonight."

Pam put her cell back down on her desk. She sat back and took a long sip of her coffee. She thought of what a great time she and Julius had together and of how she couldn't wait until they were back together again. "All right, girl, get your mind on your job."

Pam refocused and turned her attention to the files that were on her desk. She took a deep breath and opened the first file. "Well, the Delgado case is here. I certainly hope I was wrong…" Pam carefully looked through the case file scanning each page, studying every detail. She noticed right away that her speculation was correct, something that literally made her cringe. "I was really hoping that I was wrong." After about an hour of scouring through the case with meticulous resolve and a few phone calls, Pam paged Mae and asked her to come to her office.

"Sit down, please."

Mae immediately noticed the smiling and jubilant demeanor was gone from Pam's face. She immediately could sense that something was very wrong. "Pam, what is it?"

Pam, in her most serious and imposing tone, asked, "When did John give you the Delgado file as finished and ready for my review?"

"Oh, he finished that one pretty quick—I think that he gave it to me a few days ago. Did I do something wrong?"

"No, but I need you to do something. Get the personnel chief to come to my office in about ten minutes. Then get John and someone from security here in about thirty minutes…and Mae, don't discuss this with anyone."

Shocked, Mae got up and walked quickly out. "The shit is about to hit the fan," Mae whispered to herself as she picked up her phone and started arranging the meetings. It was obvious to Mae that John was in some sort of trouble, and she knew that it had something to do with the Delgado case.

Pam paced back and forth behind her desk. She was too upset to sit down, so she paced until Mae knocked on her door. "Sandy is here from personnel." Sandy walked in and closed the door behind her. In about fifteen minutes, Sandy walked out of Pam's office and without a word walked hurriedly back toward her office. Mae was curious, but did not dare ask any questions. "Whatever it is, I'm staying the hell out of the way," Mae mumbled to herself. She looked up and could see that John was making his way over to her desk. She did not want to give the impression that anything was wrong so she smiled and greeted him like always. "Hello, John, and how are you?"

John immediately asked Mae if she knew what Pam wanted, but before Mae could open her mouth, Pam opened the door to her office. "Hey, Pam, did you have a good weekend?" Pam did not smile, nor did she acknowledge John's question. John noticed that Pam was looking past him and turned around to see Curtis, one of their biggest, most intimidating security guards, walking toward them. Pam motioned for both of them to come into her office. At this point, John knew that something was wrong; he hadn't figured out yet that he was the target. Curtis instinctively knew that his purpose would be to escort someone off the property or for an arrest, so he immediately positioned himself beside Pam's desk as she sat back in her chair.

"John, please have a seat." John figured that he was in trouble for something, but at this point, hadn't figured out what.

"Pam—"

"No, John, I think that it is best that you not say anything. It's for your own good."

"But...what is..."

Pam took two files from her desk. "I put you in charge of the Delgado case." John's eyes widened and his skin moistened. "I gave you this case because I wanted to make sure that your commitment and integrity to this profession were intact."

John's mind started to race. He needed to see what Pam knew. "I'm sorry, Pam, did I miss something?"

"John, I have already warned you that it would be in your best interest not to say anything." John sat back deep into his chair. He couldn't figure out what she had on him. "Before I gave you this case, I worked the entire file myself and had already determined that Mr. Delgado was innocent. I have already prepared an order for the state to drop the case. Every piece of evidence points toward Mr. Delgado, but there is one glaring piece of evidence that you overlooked—Mr. Delgado is working for us."

John's jaw dropped. He closed his eyes tightly and shook his head from side to side.

"You put me out there on the Dent case. I knew that you were too good to miss such a critical piece of evidence. What I didn't tell you was that Mr. Dent's attorney informed me that someone had offered them a deal that involved a large sum of money. I was hoping that it wasn't you." Pam motioned for the security guard to take him away. Curtis grabbed John's arm tightly and led him out of the room. "And John, I will handle the case against you personally." John held his head down as Curtis led him quickly out of the room.

Pam took a deep breath and shook her head. She sat back in her chair struggling to hold back the tears. She had really liked John and had trusted him to do right by her. Her trust in him had almost cost her life and the freedom of a man that she had found to be one of the most caring and gentle people she had ever met. "I should feel vindicated, but instead, I just feel sad." Pam picked up the phone and called Judge Jones. "Looks like we were right. He took the bait and ran."

"I'm sorry, Pam, but you needed to know. Besides, he almost cost you your reputation…and your life." Judge Jones tried to comfort Pam. He knew how it was to find out that someone that you trust was willing to put you in harm's way just for personal gain. "Don't you worry, when his day comes in court, you will remind him of why you are in that position."

Pam thanked her friend and mentor for his support and guidance. She grabbed her things and walked out of the office. "Mae, I'm leaving for a couple of hours. Put a hold on all case files and schedule an office-wide meeting for three thirty. Anyone that has a case scheduled for that time will need to notify the court of a fifteen-minute delay. Call maintenance and have them change the lock on John's office immediately. When they are finished, lock it down and keep the key with you until I come back."

Pam walked hurriedly to the garage. She needed to get away just for a while to gather her thoughts. She knew that she would have to tell Julius what had happened and was now wishing that she had told him what she suspected earlier. She knew that he would be shocked and wondered if he would be upset with her. As Pam got into her car, she pulled out her cell phone and hit the speed dial for Julius. She quickly gathered her thoughts as the phone started to ring.

"Hey you," Julius's deep sensuous voice filled her ears.

Hearing his voice, Pam was reluctant to tell Julius what had transpired, but she knew deep down that she really had no choice. "Julius, I need to tell you something. John was dirty."

"What do you mean—dirty?"

Pam told Julius about her suspicions of John after such blatant errors were made with his case. "Julius, I had to be sure before I told you anything."

Julius was completely silent. He was not sure how to digest the information that he was hearing. "So, what you are telling me is that he withheld evidence…that my wife was murdered, and because of greed, he risked your life, almost destroyed my life, and had the power to save Denise from herself—is that what you are saying to me?"

Pam didn't know what reaction she would get from Julius, but she was somewhat surprised that he seemed so angry. "Julius, I know that you are upset, I just wanted to let you know…"

"Let me know…sounds to me that you are just trying to make yourself feel better!" Julius ended his call without another word.

Pam closed her eyes and allowed herself to cry. This was one time that she did not want to, and probably couldn't, hide her emotions. This was the second time that she had hurt this man, and she was not feeling very good about the whole situation right about now. She knew that Julius had every right to be upset, and she knew that there was a big chance that he would want absolutely nothing to do with her again—and she could not blame him. Pam pulled out of the garage and drove around the city for an hour. No music, no talking, just time to think and try to make sense of everything. She needed to keep it all in perspective; however, right now, her perspective was in suspended animation—just like a dream.

Pam looked at the clock on her dash. "Well, I better get back to the office. I have a meeting to hold."

Pam gathered herself and changed her focus to what she knew she had to do back at the office. She knew that she needed to have her game-face on at this meeting. She needed to make sure that everyone understood that this would not be tolerated on her watch, and she would make sure that John was going to be the example that no one would dare follow. As she pulled back into her parking spot, her cell phone rang. Her heart pounded as the familiar tone that she programmed for Julius pulsated from her phone.

"Hello." Pam was certainly not sure what Julius was about to say to her, but she tried to prepare herself for the worst.

"Pam, I just wanted to apologize. I really shouldn't have reacted that way, but I guess for a moment I just needed to be angry. I know that you had no control over what that idiot did, and I just want you to know that I don't blame you."

Pam breathed a sigh of relief as Julius's now calm voice gave her a sense reassurance. "That's OK, Julius; you have every right to be upset. I want you to know that I have not let myself off the hook. I should have been more diligent in my responsibilities as well. I promise you that nothing like that will ever happen again. No, not under my watch. Never again."

"I know that I caused you some undue stress with my little temper tantrum, so I have reserved a special massage for us at Body Worx tomorrow, and later, dinner at my place…about five thirty all right?"

Without hesitation Pam replied, "That's a date." Confidence in tow, Pam walked quickly back to her office and readied herself mentally to reestablish house order.

Chapter 27

Brenda smiled as she pulled up into the driveway of her condo in Atlanta. "Good to be back home again." While driving she felt the need to sleep in the bed in which she knew her sister last slept, and right now she wanted to feel closer to her and somehow feel her very essence. "Dee Dee, I'm home." Brenda walked into the closet where she had neatly hung all of her sister's clothes. She had intentionally sprayed Denise's favorite perfume on them so that she would always be reminded of her when she came into the closet. This was her shrine, a place that she could come to and talk to her sister, the place that she felt that her sister would always be. "I killed her, just like we talked about, and I made sure that they would never know that it was me.

"Yes, I know. I was very careful, and no one would ever guess that it was me. Our plan worked perfectly. I'm almost ready, big sis, almost ready."

Brenda walked out of the closet, walked over, and lay across the bed. She was now feeling a little tired but knew that sleep was the last thing that she wanted. Her adrenaline was still pumping and she could not forget how exhilarating she had felt as she thrust that paring knife into Dr. Jamison's throat. Brenda smiled as her thoughts brought unexpected moisture and excitement.

"Forget this, I'm going out!" Brenda walked back over to the closet and picked out a sexy black dress and red stilettos. She slid the dress over her head and smiled as it fell perfectly, gently caressing each curve on her body. "Damn, big-sis, you have good taste!" Brenda laughed as she grabbed her purse and headed out the door. "Oops, almost forgot." Brenda looked through her purse and smiled as she saw that she had a few of the pills that she had horded all of those years. "Now I'm ready." Brenda got into her car and headed for the Underground. She knew that the club would be filled with men looking for someone hot, and she knew that she would stand out like a sore thumb.

It took less than thirty minutes for Brenda to make it to the club. She walked in and smiled as she saw at least a dozen sets of bulging eyes checking her out, wondering what was under that tight black dress. It took less than three minutes for the first approach, which she brushed off with a flirtatious smile and gentle no. She did not want to rush, she wanted to take her time and pick out the perfect victim. She saw an empty spot at the end of the bar, walked over, and sat down. Before she could open her mouth, the bartender approached.

"The gentleman would like to buy you a drink." Brenda looked down the crowded bar to see a fairly nice-looking guy acknowledge her with a simple nod. She accepted the offer, ordering an apple martini. The bartender delivered her drink fairly quickly. She took a sip, gave the bartender her smile of approval. She looked over toward the guy who was nice enough to buy her drink. She stirred the drink with her finger, put her entire finger in her mouth, and slowly pulled it out. She smiled, put the drink on the bar, turned and walked toward the dance floor. On cue, the guy put his drink down and followed.

"Hello, I'm Curtis." Brenda lightly put a finger to his lips. She did not want to talk; she just wanted to dance, and dance she did. Brenda moved rhythmically on the dance floor, her body moving slowly and sensually to the smooth beat. Since leaving Valdosta, she had watched countless hours of videos and had methodically practiced in front of her mirror every single day; obviously she got it because all eyes were on her. Brenda's exotic look and shapely body were creating exactly what she wanted, attention. Curtis had unknowingly helped throw her coming out party, and right now, she was certainly generating the type of interest that she needed to carry out her plans. Brenda moved closer to Curtis, teasing him with the softness of her touch; his body responded instantaneously. Brenda's confidence was growing. She knew now that she didn't have to rush it, and with this type of attention, she could take her time and not risk making mistakes. Satisfied with what she had accomplished, Brenda leaned toward Curtis, kissed him lightly on the cheek, turned, and left the dance floor.

"Wait, what's your name? Can I call you?"

Brenda looked back at Curtis, winked, and left the club. She quickly walked to the parking lot, found her car, and drove away. She did not want Curtis or any other inquisitive minds following her.

Brenda's quick success at the club had helped change her mind about killing so soon after getting rid of Dr. Jamison. "Impulse can get you caught, and they will never catch me—I'm too damn smart."

Brenda turned up her music and headed for her place in Buckhead. She needed to make sure that no one had followed her, and the drive would give her a chance to calm herself down from the excitement that she was feeling from dancing at the club.

"That was fucking exhilarating. I had those poor bastards drooling all over themselves." Brenda was almost amazed at how easy it had been to draw that type of attention. Denise had always told her that she was beautiful, but because of the mental turmoil that she was going through, she had never really grasped or noticed the wonderful thing that her mother and father's mixed marriage had actually produced. She had missed out on the attention that she would have gotten because of her looks. Since the age of nine, she was all but isolated—a hidden treasure. As Brenda turned the corner she noticed a young couple standing on the corner; obviously in a heated discussion. As Brenda passed she saw the young lady slap the guy, get in her car, and drive off. Looking through her rearview mirror, she saw the guy turn and start walking back to the club. She made a quick left into another parking lot, turned around, and drove back toward the guy.

"Hey, I saw that you were having a little problem with your girl—need a lift?"

The young man walked over. "Do you always pick up strangers?"

Brenda smiled. "Only those that just got their ass kicked by a lady." They both laughed as the guy walked around and got in. "I knew when you didn't hit her back that you were probably harmless."

"OK, I'm busted. My name is Ken."

"OK, Ken, I'm Brenda. Where can I take you?"

"My condo is right off the Parkway. Are you sure you don't mind?"

"It's no problem. I think that you would have done the same for me."

Ken looked at Brenda, realizing how stunning she was. "Yes, but I don't think anyone in their right mind would ever put you out of the car and make you walk."

Brenda followed Ken's directions to his condo. As they pulled up Ken began to thank her for being so kind. "Brenda, you are so nice. Not many people would do this in Atlanta; it is much too dangerous. Let me give you something for gas." Ken pulled out his wallet and grabbed a one hundred dollar bill.

Brenda shook her head no. "Now why would you insult me like that?"

Ken was surprised; most women that he knew would have grabbed the money and run. "I didn't mean to insult you; I was just trying to show my appreciation for your kindness."

Brenda smiled. "I know, but I really don't need your money."

Somewhat embarrassed, Ken opened the door and got out. "Thanks for the ride. Maybe I will see you another time." As Brenda started to drive off, Ken ran back up to the car. "Hey, could I at least invite you up for a drink before you go? …And don't worry. I'm harmless, remember."

Brenda looked at Ken, smiled, and agreed to have a drink with him.

"I have a reserved parking spot next to my car." Ken pointed over toward a black Corvette. Brenda looked back up at him as if to say yeah—right. "Don't trip—my lady friend had invited me out and came by to pick me up. I have my own, thank you."

They both laughed as Brenda parked her car. Ken opened the car door for Brenda. His eyes almost popped out of his head as Brenda opened her legs to get out of the car. Her dress had pulled up and he could see every bit of her neatly shaved, not so privates. Ken had to catch his breath and strain to act inconspicuous. "Take that!" Brenda thought to herself. She knew that Ken had gotten an eyeful and would be bursting at the seam by the time she finished her drink.

Ken opened the door to his condo and invited Brenda in. He was obviously proud of his place, and he had every right to be. Brenda looked around and realized that Ken obviously was successful at something.

"Please, have a seat." Ken pointed toward his sitting area. There was a plush white leather sofa and recliner positioned nicely in front of a huge plasma screen television perched menacingly on the wall. "Now, what can I get you to drink?"

Brenda wasn't a big drinker, but she had watched enough videos to know what the going thing was. "Patron." Ken was happy to oblige and quickly came back carrying a tray with two glasses filled with ice and a bottle of Patron. "You have a really nice place, Ken."

"Thank you—so Brenda, let me guess, you are a model."

Brenda knew that the questions would start, but she was ready. "No, I'm not a model."

"Well, you sure could be one." Ken was captivated by Brenda's seductive demeanor, and yet intrigued by her air of innocence. He could tell that there was something about her, but he could not put his finger on it. "Well, what do you do?"

Brenda smiled. "Right now, I'm in research."

Ken poured the Patron into the glasses. "Thanks for having a drink with me, and especially for being sweet enough to give me a ride."

Brenda smiled and took a sip of her drink. She knew that Ken wasn't as innocent as he purported to be since he had filled her glass to the rim, expecting her to get tipsy and giving him a better chance of getting lucky.

"Let me turn on some music." Ken reached over to grab the remote to his stereo system. When he turned his head, Brenda intentionally spilled some of her drink on her dress.

"Crap, I spilled some on my dress."

"Let me go get you a towel." Ken jumped up and left the room. Brenda quickly reached into her purse and grabbed four capsules. She twisted the capsules and dumped the contents into Ken's drink, being careful not to spill any of the white powder on the tray. She stirred the drink with her finger and quickly put the empty capsules in her purse just as Ken reappeared and handed her a towel.

"Thank you...See, models would not be so clumsy."

Ken smiled as he noticed Brenda's lightly dimpled cheeks. "You are a gorgeous lady. I hope that this won't be the last time that I see you." Ken turned on his stereo.

Brenda was surprised to hear mellow music versus loud thunderous booming. The music actually reminded her of what her father used to listen to. "Oh yeah, this will make it easy," Brenda thought to herself. Brenda sipped slowly on her drink as Ken began his small talk routine, waiting on the drink to have its effect on Brenda. What he didn't notice, however, was the effect that his tainted drink was having on him. It wasn't long before his speech was slurring badly and he was having trouble focusing. Ken shook his head trying to shake off the effect of the pills.

"Dang, it feels like I've been drinking all—" Before he could finish his sentence, Brenda walked over and straddled his body. She leaned over and kissed Ken passionately as his body sank deep into the soft leather. Ken stared blankly as his mind and body suspended in a medicated fog.

"That's why I never took that shit—this is exactly how they wanted me to be." Brenda started getting a bit irritated, thinking back on all the years of condescending bull that she had to endure back in Valdosta. She remembered how long she faked being medicated and allowed the staff to touch her in places that she should never had been touched, say things to her that should never have been said, and do things to her that no child should have to endure.

Brenda ran her fingers along the side of Ken's neck, feeling the slow steady pulsation of his carotid artery. "This will be too dang messy, honey—why don't we try something a little different." Brenda unbuckled Ken's jeans and pulled them down to his knees. She ran her hands up and down the inside of his thigh, finding her spot up near his groin. "There it is; just where the books at the library said it would be." Brenda had found the strong pulsation of Ken's femoral artery. Brenda got up, walked over and grabbed the towel that Ken had brought her. She reached into her purse and grabbed the thin lock-blade. She turned and walked back over to Ken. She stuffed one end of the towel in his mouth, making sure that he would not be able to make any noise other than maybe a muffled scream.

Brenda stood next to Ken, reached down, and quickly found her mark. With surgeon-like precision, she pushed the small knife deep into his thigh right above the femoral artery, then with wrist action only, pushed down hard, completely severing the artery inside the thigh. Brenda was careful not to cause too much damage externally; she wanted the wound to be neat and most of the bleeding to be internal. She withdrew the blade and quickly applied pressure with the other end of the towel. She was careful not to touch the white sofa or anything that may leave a trace of her being there. Ken's thigh and leg began to swell as the blood poured freely from the artery. Brenda quickly pulled his jeans back up, zipped and buttoned them closed. She watched intensely as Ken's eyes slowly closed, and his essence of life drifted away. She took his index finger, dabbed it lightly on the blood-stained sofa, and traced the initials "LTD-R".

Brenda looked carefully around the room, noting every single thing that she may have touched. She checked to make sure that no blood was on her hand and that she had not left any prints on the white sofa. She grabbed her glass and walked to the sink. She used a dish towel to turn the faucet on and wash the glass. She put the glass in the dishwasher so that no one would suspect that more than one person had been there. Brenda looked around one final time before she used the dish towel to open the door and leave.

She walked quickly to her car and backed out. As she was leaving the parking lot, she noticed a car pulling in and parking next to Ken's Corvette. It was the same car that she had seen earlier, the one his girlfriend had been driving. Brenda slammed her fist down on the center console. She was upset that she had almost been caught. "I should have followed my first mind and just gone home. That almost cost me everything." Brenda sped away toward her place in Buckhead. She knew that she had been lucky this time. She also knew that she had passed the point of no return. There could be no stopping or quitting at this point. She was committed to finish what she had started, but she also realized that she could not afford to make mistakes. "I will have to get better…much better."

Brenda stopped in front of her condo, sat, and stared at the front door. She wondered what it would be like if her sister were still alive. She tried to imagine opening the door and having Denise welcome her with conversation of how her day had gone.

"We never got a chance, Dee-Dee, not a chance." The familiar taste of blood filled Brenda's mouth. Without realizing it, she had bit down harder than normal on the inside of her lip. She opened the door of her car and spit out a small chunk of skin. As always, Brenda scanned the area as she walked toward her front door to make sure that no one noticed when she was arriving. She was careful not to be predictable; she did not want anyone to be able to gauge when she could be expected to be in one place or the other.

Convinced that prying eyes were not watching, she quickly unlocked her door and walked in. Brenda started undressing the moment she walked through her door, leaving a trail of clothes behind her as she made her way to the bedroom. This had been a very long day, and she was starting to feel the effects of no sleep and from being mentally fatigued from all that had happened. "Two kills…one day…not too bad." Brenda's body and mind finally gave in; she fell asleep almost as her head hit the pillow, with blood on her lips and a smile on her face.

* * *

Brenda sat straight up in the bed. "What the..." She thought that she had been dreaming, but the loud pounding she heard was not a dream; someone was knocking loudly on her front door and alternately ringing her door bell. Brenda grabbed a night gown from the top dresser drawer and quickly ran to see what was going on. She looked through the peep-hole and gasped as she saw two uniformed officers at her door.

"Shit—I'm caught!" Brenda stepped back from the door for a second and took a deep breath. She quickly went over things in her mind trying to see what mistake she could have made and wondered who could have seen her. She knew that she was busted, so she slowly opened the door.

"Miss..." The police officer looked at her and reached for the door knob. "Is everything all right? Do you need some assistance?"

Confused, Brenda responded, "I'm fine. What is the problem, officer?"

The policeman was looking around Brenda as if to see if anyone else was standing behind her. Brenda could see that he had his hand on his weapon, and she was all but ready to be arrested. "You have dried blood on your lips. Are you all right? Is someone here hurting you?"

Brenda looked at the officer and smiled widely. "Oh no, I bit my lip last night. There is no one here but me."

The officer seemed to lessen his level of concern, but Brenda was still on edge since she had no idea why they were there. "Mr. Sims, your neighbor, backed into your car this morning. He tried knocking at your door to let you know, but didn't get an answer, so he was honest enough to call us to make a report."

Brenda's nerves finally calmed when she realized that they knew absolutely nothing about what she had done. "Well, that was nice of him; most people around here would have driven off and not said a word."

The officer smiled. "Yes, good honest people are getting harder to find." The officers wrote down some information for Brenda so that she could give it to her insurance company and quickly left.

Brenda watched as the policemen drove away. She was feeling

quite a bit of anxiety. "There is no way that I'm going to be put away again. I'm going to get this done and leave for awhile." Brenda walked over to her sofa, grabbed the remote, and turned on the television. As she flipped through the channels, she stopped on a news channel that was showing a picture of Julius Dent. "Well, look who's in the news." They were reporting the corruption and arrest of John Franks, the Assistant District Attorney.

Brenda could feel herself getting angry. "Those bastards are the reason my sister is dead. I'll kill them all…yes, I will!" Brenda flipped from news station to news station, listening and taking in every detail of the story. She wanted as much information as possible so she soaked in as much as she could. One report was by Cynthia LaMay, and her news footage showed a good close-up shot of the front door of Dent Enterprises. Brenda stared at the silver and black number pad anchored securely in the brick surrounding the door. "The envelope with the code and key!" Brenda remembered that one of the things Denise had put in the safe deposit box was an envelope labeled "Dent Enterprises" with a key and a four digit code inside. "That has to be the key to the door and security code…I wonder if he ever changed them?"

Brenda's eyes grew big with excitement. She couldn't wait to check and see if this was her way to get to Julius. She knew that if she could get into his office, she would be able to find out everything she needed to know and be able to plan his death much quicker than she had expected.

Chapter 28

Brenda stared at the bold letters etched neatly across the double glass doors. Without provocation, the familiar taste of her blood warned her of the anxiety that was building inside, begging to be released. She knew that she had to be extra careful; she simply could not afford to make a mistake. "Dent Enterprises..." Brenda repeated the name in her head over and over again until the name was nothing more than a tone, a sound pounding menacingly in her mind. Brenda looked around checking out every window, every door. She paid special attention to any cars passing by, making sure that no one was stopping or looking as if they were watching. She decided to drive the block once more just to make sure.

"What am I worried about? They have no idea, not a clue that I even exist." Brenda was right. The detectives in Valdosta were not even close to putting the pieces of the puzzle together, and the locals had no reason to suspect Brenda's vengeful intent. Convinced that she was ready, Brenda parked at the far end of the parking lot. She got out of her car and walked quickly to the front door of Dent Enterprises. Looking intently at the security pad, she noticed that the red armed light was on and knew that if the code had been changed, the key would make no difference. Brenda took a deep breath and slowly pushed the four numbers. Almost immediately, the red light went off and the green light illuminated brightly. Her heart pounded loudly as she quickly put the key inside the lock, and to her surprise, the lock had not been changed. Brenda opened the door and walked inside, carefully locking the door behind her.

As Brenda walked quickly toward the back offices, tears of anger filled her eyes. She realized that she was actually in the office where her sister had worked—the same place that, as far as she was concerned, contributed to her death. Brenda gathered her thoughts and regained her focus. She was here for one thing and one thing only. Although there was very little light, she quickly found Julius's office, walked in, and closed the door behind her. Brenda did not immediately turn on the light; she stood there in the darkness, almost reluctant or maybe even unwilling to go any further. She knew that once she turned the lights on, she would be at the point of no return with her intent to carry out the revenge of her sister's death, and at the same time, she knew she had no choice.

Brenda flipped the light switch and paused as her eyes adjusted to the sudden brightness. She slowly walked around the office, carefully detailing every single piece of furniture, artwork, and even each piece of paper stacked neatly on his desk. Brenda walked over and gently touched the soft leather of Julius's chair and sighed as the coolness of the leather triggered pleasure sensors in her body.

"Whoa, girl, got to get busy." Brenda quickly pushed her inhibitions aside and started carefully rifling through the papers both on and in Julius's desk; it didn't take long for her to find what she was looking for written down on Julius's day planner. As she carefully jotted down notes, Brenda noticed the message light flashing on the phone. She picked up the receiver and pushed the message button. She carefully listened to the voice message.

"This is Renee at Body Worx…just wanted to confirm the couple's massage for tomorrow at six o'clock and to ask if you have any special requests. You will be in the waterfall room, and it will be ready by five thirty so you can come a little early if you would like. Anyway, I will call your cell number as well, so if you need anything, just let me know. If I don't hear from you, I will just prepare the usual….and I won't forget your herbal tea this time."

Brenda smiled; she knew that she had an opportunity and the time to perfect a plan. She carefully put everything back in its place and walked out of the office. She walked cautiously to the front door, pausing to make sure that no one was around the building entrance. After a few minutes, she was convinced that it was safe to leave. She locked the door, carefully activated the alarm system, and quickly walked back to her car.

Brenda was amazed at how easy this had been. She even toyed with the idea of going back and trashing the place, but quickly dismissed that idea since it would tip them that someone had access to the office and put everyone on alert. No, she knew that she had to stay focused and not get overconfident.

"Now is not the time to start making stupid mistakes!" Brenda thought back to all of those long hours that she had spent at the library researching and studying serial killers. She knew that most of them developed a sense of invincibility that led to mistakes and of course, eventual capture. She knew that she could be smarter, more calculating and cunning than anyone could ever imagine. "Besides, who would suspect me? I am like a ghost, an apparition—I don't even exist!" Brenda looked at herself in the rear-view mirror and smiled as the image of Dent Enterprises slowly disappeared from her sight.

CHAPTER 29

Julius looked impatiently at his watch, almost comically urging the second hand to move faster. "I don't know why I'm so antsy about my date with Pam. Guess I was looking forward to this more than I thought. Damn, I haven't felt this way in a long time…" It was four o'clock and he had let everyone off, so Julius was surprised when Carolyn knocked on his office door. "I thought everyone was gone; what are you still doing here?"

Carolyn smiled. "Well, I was about to leave, but you have a visitor, and I wanted to make sure that you wouldn't need anything else." Julius stared at Carolyn with his "who the heck is it" look. Carolyn opened the door wider.

"Pam, what are you doing here?"

Before she could answer, Carolyn interrupted, "You two have a good weekend. I'll lock up on my way out." Julius smiled as Carolyn turned and walked away.

Pam walked slowly toward Julius. "Sorry to intrude, Mr. Dent, but anticipation got the best of me. I hope you don't mind me stopping by so…"

Without a word, Julius grabbed Pam and pulled her body tightly against his. "This is scary," he whispered in her ear. "I could barely wait to see you…" Julius kissed Pam tenderly, picked her up in his arms, and carried her over to his desk. Pam wrapped her legs tightly around his waist, allowing Julius to feel the heat radiating from between her thighs. Julius sat Pam gently down on his desk and slowly pulled away from their steamy embrace. Pam looked down at the obvious bulge stretching menacingly across Julius's otherwise flawless slack's pocket.

"So, I see you are happy to see me too."

Julius ran his hands slowly from Pam's knees to the inner parts of her thighs, being careful to come as close as possible without touching what Pam most wanted him to touch. Pam closed her eyes as the sensation from his soft touch caused her to tremble in anticipation. "No, we will have to wait until after our appointment at the spa; if we get started—we will never make it in time."

Pam reluctantly agreed and pulled Julius back close to her, wrapping her legs back around his waist. "Julius, I…"

Before Pam could say another word, Julius shook his head no and kissed her so passionately that she knew that she did not have to apologize and all had been forgiven. This was the moment that both of them knew that their relationship was going to the next level. The tears in their eyes said it all.

Pam wiped the tears from Julius's eyes. She instinctively knew that words did not have to be expressed, and knew that Julius must feel for her the same that she felt for him. Pam grabbed her stomach and closed her eyes.

"What's wrong?" Julius was worried that maybe Pam was feeling ill.

Pam looked at Julius and smiled. "Nothing is wrong. Right now, everything is so very right."

Julius looked at his watch. "We better go now or we will be late. Why don't you just leave your car here. We will pick it up tomorrow."

Pam nodded in agreement as they both walked hand-in-hand out of the office. As Julius locked the front door and set the alarm, he stared back in through the doors. "What's wrong?" Pam noticed Julius's stare.

"Oh, nothing…just felt funny for a moment." Julius wasn't being totally honest. What he actually had felt was a strong desire not to leave the office—almost a beckoning for him to stay. Julius shook off his apprehension, grabbed Pam's hand, and walked toward his car. Julius opened the door for Pam and smiled as she settled back into the seat. He hurried around and joined Pam in the car. "Ready for the first part of your treat?"

Pam smiled. "Hmm, so you have a part two as well—I feel special."

Julius reached over and put his hand on her thigh. "Special indeed!" Julius pulled out of the parking lot and headed for Body Worx.

Pam looked down at Julius's strong hand and thought back to how this whole thing began. She closed her eyes, trying hard to hold back tears as she thought of how she had publicly ridiculed this kind and gentle man—how she had all but destroyed his reputation at a time when his whole life had been torn apart. She wondered what kind of man could find this level of forgiveness in his heart and share his love with the same person that had treated him so cruelly.

"Hey, you OK over there?" Julius's instincts told him that Pam was having a moment.

"Just sitting here thinking of how lucky I am, and how wonderful I feel when I'm around you. Julius, I—"

Julius stopped Pam in mid-sentence. "I don't want you all worked up before your massage. Trust me—there will be plenty of time for passionate apologies later." Pam smiled as Julius turned into the parking lot at Body Worx. "All right, Ms. Cooper, I guess this is our coming out party."

Pam put her hand over her mouth as she realized that this was the first time that she and Julius would be seen out together as a couple. "Are you sure, Julius? You know how cruel people can be."

Julius got out of the car, walked around and opened the door for Pam. He reached for her hand and gently helped her out of the car. "Very sure, Ms. Cooper, very sure indeed."

Julius was not so shocked to notice people staring as he and Pam walked hand-in-hand through the front doors. They both knew that most would recognize them and all would be surprised that they were now a couple. As they approached the desk, the greeter immediately escorted the two of them back to the dressing areas.

"Mr. Dent, we have the Waterfall room ready for you. I hope that you don't mind, but someone from your office came by a little earlier and left you a basket."

Julius looked at Pam and shook his head. "Those ladies don't miss a thing."

Pam smirked. "They better take care of you, or they will have to deal with me." They both laughed as Pam disappeared into the ladies dressing and shower room. Julius quickly turned and walked into the men's dressing room. He was anticipating Renee's magic hands, but mostly anticipating enjoying his first massage together with Pam. He quickly undressed and took a short hot shower to help his muscles relax.

Pam, on the other hand, could not resist the temptation of the sauna, so after her shower she made a beeline to the sauna to sneak a few minutes of the intense heat before she met back up with Julius. Pam opened the sauna door and was happy to see that she would have it all to herself. "I'll just sit here for a minute." Pam was about to lower the towel from around her when the door to the sauna opened. She was somewhat disappointed as someone else walked in and sat down next to her.

"Hello." The young lady spoke to Pam in a very low, almost inaudible tone.

Before Pam could speak, the young lady got right back up and walked out. "Hmmm, that was strange," Pam thought to herself. "Oh well, maybe she forgot something. I'll just stay for a few more minutes, and then go see my man." Pam felt good saying those words to herself; in fact, saying those words made her feel better than she had ever felt before.

Julius sat patiently in the sitting area right outside of the massage room. He sipped slowly on his hot herbal tea as the soothing sound of waterfalls filled his ears. There was a gentle tap on the door. "Come in." Julius's voice was indicative of his level of relaxation.

As the door opened, Renee walked in. "Hello, Mr. Dent, happy to see you again. I have something special planned for you and your guest, so I am going to go ahead and prepare the tables for you two."

Julius grabbed his shoulder as to be in pain. "Yeah, looks like you may have to spend some extra time with me this time."

Renee laughed. "Don't worry—I will take good care of you. I will go over to the other side to see if your guest is ready." Renee opened the door to the massage room and walked in just as the door from the opposite side was opening. Before Renee could speak, the young lady put her finger to her lips, motioning for her to be quiet. Renee closed the door behind her as the young lady approached.

"I want to surprise him and be all oiled up when he walks in the room."

Renee smiled and nodded in agreement. She thought to herself how this person really looked familiar, but couldn't quite place her. "Lucky fool, bet I could rock him better," Renee thought to herself. "Wouldn't have thought that this was his type though—oh well." Renee was surprised as the young lady took off her robe, revealing a new, perfect body. "OK, let me go over and get some sheets for the table." Renee walked over to the warming bins and pulled out a few warm sheets. She walked over and covered one of the massage tables, then returned to a separate warming bin that contained her massage oils.

Julius had finished a second cup of tea and was getting a bit anxious. He wondered what was taking so long, so he walked over to the door of the massage room and gently knocked...there was no answer. Julius knocked a little harder and called out Renee's name...still no answer. Julius tried to turn the knob on the door only to find out that it was locked. "Well, she must have gone over through the other side to find Pam, but it has been a bit too long. Hope everything is all right."

Concerned, Julius walked out of the room to find a staff member to check on Pam. On his way back up to the front area, he couldn't help but notice this young lady that had turned and looked back at him as she was leaving the building. "She kind of looks familiar, but I would remember that one!" Julius thought to himself as he finally found one of the staff members.

Julius explained the situation and the young lady grabbed a set of keys and walked back to the waterfall room with Julius. The young lady knocked on the door and called out for Renee. There was no answer so the young lady unlocked and opened the door. She walked through the door and immediately screamed. She turned and ran out of the room, screaming for help at the top of her lungs.

Julius stood there, stunned and staring at the massive amount of blood that had pooled beneath the massage table. He could not believe that this was happening all over again. He did not have the strength to pull the blood-stained sheet from the body that lay motionless on the table, so he just stood there, staring in disbelief. Julius's heart pounded loudly as he watched the blood flow down the grout of the once perfect white tile floor. Thoughts and images of Tiara rushed through his mind like the force of a hurricane. Struggling to keep his balance, Julius staggered backward into the wall, leaning hard against it just to keep from falling. He did not know what he was going to do. Though the sheet still covered the body, he knew that it must be Pam.

"Why?" Julius screamed. As additional staff raced in behind him, the door on the opposite side of the room burst open. Julius's eyes filled with tears as Pam stood there in the doorway. Pam stared at the blood-stained sheet covering the body, then looked up at Julius. She rushed over to Julius as he began to sink slowly to the floor.

"I thought it was you...I thought it was you." Julius was relieved that Pam was safe, and he squeezed her in his arms with true earnest; then almost simultaneously, his eyes focused back on the still-covered body lying hauntingly under the sheet. "Oh my God, it must be Renee!"

Julius's heart sank and he began to openly sob. He couldn't stand the thought of another life gone, wasted. "Pam, what is happening?" Julius's strong and confident demeanor was for the moment absent. Now he looked to Pam for strength and comfort.

Pam gathered her thoughts, stood up, and tightened the white terry-cloth robe around her waist. "Everyone needs to move back out of the room. We don't want to disturb anything before the police get here." Surprisingly, the small crowd responded quickly and moved back outside of the room. Pam stood there wondering if this was meant for her. She wondered if John had somehow arranged this or if it was just a coincidence. Pam looked down at Julius. "They are here."

Three police officers walked into the room. One of the officers immediately called in on his radio for a supervisor. "I think you better get over here. We have a situation that is going to call for some media intervention."

Pam walked over to the officer. "We will wait for the supervisor and detectives before we change clothes. We don't want there to be any confusion or indication that we have anything to hide from you." The officer acknowledged Pam with a nod. He had immediately recognized both her and Julius and knew that she understood protocol.

The officer walked over to the body, being careful not to disturb any potential evidence. He lifted the sheet from one side, being extra careful to shield the body from anyone else's view. He noted a single puncture wound to the neck and the letters LTD-R in blood across the victim's forehead. As he lowered the sheet, the shift supervisor and detectives walked through the door. He quickly walked over to them.

"Looks like we have a serial killer." The detectives walked over, lifted the sheet, and viewed the body. They too were careful not to allow anyone else to see the body. After a few minutes, they walked over to Pam and Julius. "Ms. Cooper, Mr. Dent, we need to talk."

* * *

Brenda stared intently at the television as the caption "BREAKING NEWS" scrolled across the screen. She was disappointed as Cynthia LaMay reported the murder at Body Worx.

She was anxious to hear them mention Pam and Julius, but that never came. The only thing that made her smile was the mention that the murder appeared to be the work of a serial killer. "The details of this murder and those that make the authorities link similarities to other recent murders have not been released; however, detectives were definitive in their reference to a serial killer."

Brenda rubbed her hands together, wondering if she had made mistakes that would lead the authorities to her. She played back in her mind her sudden decision to target someone else instead of Pam and Julius, yet getting close enough so there would be no question that this was a message. She wondered whether she had made mistakes and whether she would get caught before she could carry out her plan. "No, it was perfect—I have to stop second-guessing myself!"

Brenda turned up the volume on the television as she finished packing her bag. She walked carefully through each room, making sure that there was nothing that would tip her involvement, just in case the authorities were smart enough to find her. "I'm giving them far too much credit." Brenda laughed loudly as she carefully scanned her checklist, making sure that she had prepared both condos for her planned absence. "I'm going to throw so many twists at them, they will never figure this one out…and when I'm ready, Mr. Dent, you and your gal-pal will die together!"

Brenda turned off the light and looked out the front window of her condo as usual, checking for activity before she walked out. After a moment or two, she felt that it was clear for her to leave. She carefully locked the door and walked briskly to her car. She sat in the car for two or three minutes, carefully scanning for nosey neighbors. Relieved, she drove slowly away. Brenda looked down at the book that she had left on the passenger seat of her car. The title read "The Town That Dreaded Sundown."

"You just think that you dreaded sundown. Just wait until I'm finished." Brenda made her way to the interstate and drove west toward Texarkana.

Made in the USA
Charleston, SC
08 February 2013